How *Did* She Feel About Chase's Offer?

Her stomach jumped at the question, followed by a peculiar, almost traitorous warmth that spread through her.

Could she actually be attracted to Chase? On more than simply the detached level of a woman catching a glimpse of a good-looking man?

Could the attraction go deeper? Could she actually be considering saying yes to his proposition? To becoming his mistress?

A skittering of nerves joined the heat flowing through her bloodstream. She'd never been a man's mistress before, never been in a relationship based solely on sex. She and Chase had nothing in common other than her father's company. He wanted her for two reasons only—to look good on his arm at business gatherings and to satisfy him in bed.

And darned if that idea wasn't becoming more appealing by the minute.

Dear Reader,

As soon as I started writing my November 2006 Silhouette Desire title, *Bedded Then Wed,* I knew that the hero's brother would have to get his own story. With a name like Chase Ramsey, how could I resist?

I wasn't sure just what kind of trouble he should find himself in, though. Then it hit me—blackmail. I'd never done a revenge book before, and it sounded like great fun to me. And what could be better—or sexier—than being *Blackmailed into Bed?* Needless to say, I quite enjoyed writing Chase and Elena's story, and I hope you'll enjoy them, too.

Watch for Elena's sister's story, too, which will be out soon. Because a woman like Alandra Sanchez deserves a very special hero.

All my best!
Heidi Betts

P.S. Don't forget to visit www.heidibetts.com for information about all my books.

HEIDI BETTS

BLACKMAILED INTO BED

Silhouette®
Desire

Published by Silhouette Books
America's Publisher of Contemporary Romance

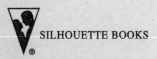

SILHOUETTE BOOKS

RECYCLED PAPER

ISBN-13: 978-0-373-76779-3
ISBN-10:   0-373-76779-X

BLACKMAILED INTO BED

Copyright © 2007 by Heidi Betts

Visit Silhouette Books at www.eHarlequin.com

Printed in U.S.A.

Books by Heidi Betts

Silhouette Desire

Bought by a Millionaire #1638
Blame It on the Blackout #1662
When the Lights Go Down #1686
Seven-Year Seduction #1709
Mr. and Mistress #1709
Bedded Then *Wed* #1761
Blackmailed into Bed #1779

HEIDI BETTS

An avid romance reader since junior high school, Heidi knew early on that she wanted to write these wonderful stories of love and adventure. It wasn't until her freshman year of college, however, when she spent the entire night reading a romance novel instead of studying for finals, that she decided to take the road less traveled and follow her dream. In addition to reading and writing romance, she is the founder of her local Romance Writers of America chapter and has a tendency to take injured and homeless animals of every species into her Central Pennsylvania home.

Heidi loves to hear from readers. You can write to her at P.O. Box 99, Kylertown, PA 16847 (an SASE is appreciated, but not necessary) or e-mail heidi@heidibetts.com. And be sure to visit www.heidibetts.com for news and information about upcoming books.

To my wonderful readers, who are—without question—the greatest in the world. So many of you, so sweet and supportive. Thank you for your letters and e-mails and kind words of encouragement when I see you in person. You remind me on a daily basis of why I love my job so much, and keep me going on those long, dreary days when the words won't seem to come.

This one's for you!

One

Elena Sanchez looked up and down the long hallway, her heels clicking on the expensively tiled floor as she moved. There was no one behind the desk where she assumed a receptionist would normally sit, but then, it was lunch time. Even she had sneaked away from the office to come over here.

She glanced at the doors as she passed, searching for the one she needed, for the name of the man she had to see, whether she wanted to or not. And she really didn't want to. If her father wasn't desperate—if she wasn't desperate on her father's behalf—she probably would have gone the rest of her life without bumping into Chase Ramsey.

She certainly wouldn't have made a point of tracking him down.

When she saw his name printed in black block letters

on the gold door plate at the end of the hall, her stomach jumped and she had the sudden urge to turn and run. But she'd made up her mind to do this, so she would.

Raising a hand, she knocked, and then wiped her damp palms on the sides of her red linen, knee-length skirt so he wouldn't realize how nervous she was if he shook her hand.

She heard mumbling from the other side, perhaps even a curse, followed by a grumbled, "Come in."

Twisting the knob, she pushed the dark wooden door open and stepped inside.

His office was huge, encompassing three large plate glass windows that overlooked downtown Austin. An oriental rug and two dark green overstuffed leather armchairs filled the space in front of his wide cherrywood desk.

Behind that desk, Chase Ramsey sat scribbling notes while he held the phone to his ear and carried on a somewhat heated conversation with whoever was on the other end of the line. He didn't bother looking up, even though she knew he must have heard her enter.

Not presumptuous enough to take a seat until invited, Elena stayed where she was, standing just inside the office door, clenching and unclenching her fingers around the strap of her purse that hung at her side.

He was as handsome as she remembered. Darn it. But in a darker, much more mature way—she hadn't seen him since they were teenagers.

His hair was as black as midnight, cut short, with just a hint of curl that fell over his forehead. And from what she could see above the desk, he filled his dark gray, expensive, tailored suit to perfection. Broad shoulders, expansive chest, tanned hands that looked strong enough to lift a small building.

Or stroke across a woman's thigh.

Oh, Lord. Where had that come from? She clutched the strap of her handbag more tightly and fought the urge to fan her face. Butterflies were flying in rapid formation through her stomach, making her weak in the knees.

So he had big hands. Big, dark, impressive hands. The fact that she'd noticed—and was apparently quite distracted by them—meant nothing. Except perhaps that it had been awhile since she'd had any decent, attractive male company. Even longer since a man had been near her thighs—with his hands or anything else.

She heard a click and blinked, raising her gaze back to the man behind the desk. While she'd been fantasizing about long, masculine fingers sliding beneath the hem of her skirt, Chase Ramsey had apparently finished his conversation and was now staring at her with an impatient, annoyed glint in his sharp blue eyes.

"Can I help you with something?" he asked.

Taking a deep breath and steeling her nerves, she stepped forward to stand between the two guest chairs angled in front of his desk.

"Yes, actually," she said, brushing a lock of hair behind her ear before resting her palm on the high back of one of the chairs. "My name is Elena Sanchez, and I'd like to talk to you about your interest in Sanchez Restaurant Supply Company."

She knew the exact moment he recognized her. Not just the name of her father's company as one he was in the process of taking over, but recognized *her*. Her name and possibly her features, if he remembered anything about her from all those years ago.

His eyes turned hard and dark, his mouth tightening to a thin, flat line. He dropped the pen in his right hand on top of the papers he'd been working on and leaned back in his chair, resting his elbows on the padded arms and steepling his fingers in front of him as he rocked back and forth, back and forth.

Inwardly, she cringed. Judging by his reaction to her presence, his memory was as impressive as his physical attributes.

And his disdain was justified, she knew. Two decades ago, she'd been a spoiled, high-strung teenager, and had treated a lot of people badly, Chase included.

Not that her youth could be used as an excuse. Everyone makes mistakes when they're kids, and sometimes those mistakes have to be paid for or made right.

This, Elena decided, was her punishment for having had a lousy attitude as an adolescent—coming face-to-face with Chase Ramsey again, and essentially having to grovel in an attempt to help her father save the family business.

It might not be easy, but she would step up and take her lumps like the mature adult she'd grown into.

A phone rang out in the hallway, but Chase ignored it. He just kept rocking in his high-priced leather desk chair, staring at her as though he could see straight through to her soul.

And maybe he could. She felt exposed down to the bone. She might as well have been standing in the middle of his office stark naked, instead of in one of her most professional dress suits.

The red linen skirt and matching jacket over a low-cut

white blouse always made her feel powerful and in control. She'd worn it purposely this morning, knowing she would be facing the lion in his den.

But now she realized her choice of clothing made absolutely no difference. She could have been wearing a suit of armor and would be no less nervous about standing in front of Chase Ramsey, waiting for him to strip a few layers of skin off her hide or order her out of his office without even letting her explain her reason for being there.

Instead, he lifted one black eyebrow and sat forward again, the corners of his mouth twisting in the grim mockery of a smile.

"Elena Sanchez," he murmured coldly, pushing slowly to his feet and moving around his desk. "Now, there's a name I never thought I'd hear again. Can't say I ever expected you to saunter into my office, either."

He paused directly in front of her, with fewer than three feet of space between them. The air was thick and tense, and Elena found her lungs straining for breath with him standing in such close proximity.

Leaning back against the edge of the desk, he crossed his arms over his chest and pierced her with that glacial blue glare.

"I take it you're here to beg me not to buy out your daddy's business," he said, his tone only a notch above patronizing. "Sorry, sweetheart, but I didn't build Ramsey Corporation into a multimillion dollar company by falling for long lashes and a nice pair of legs."

He let his gaze travel blatantly down her body, past her breasts, her waist, her hips, until they caught and held on the expanse of leg left visible below the hem of her skirt, which fell just above her knees.

"No matter how shapely they might be," he added before dragging his eyes reluctantly back to her face.

It was her turn to raise a brow. She dropped her purse on the seat of one of the guest chairs and took a more defensive stance.

"I'm not here to *beg* you for anything. I came to *speak* with you about a business issue that's important to my family. And whether or not you find my eyelashes and legs attractive is completely inconsequential. We're both adults; we should be able to sit down and talk in a calm, professional manner without you ogling me like a parolee on his first visit to a strip club after twenty years in solitary confinement."

The muscles in Chase's cheeks twitched, and it took all of his willpower to keep from letting that twitch spread into a full-blown grin.

It had been almost twenty years since he'd seen or spoken to Elena Sanchez. Frankly, he'd never given a damn if he ever saw or spoke to her again. She was one of those painful memories from childhood that still oozed and bled if he let down his guard long enough to peel back the curtain between present and past.

Thankfully, he didn't do that very often. He hadn't thought about Elena in years. Not even, surprisingly, when he'd begun the process of buying out her father's restaurant supply company. To Chase, it was just another smart business move; the kind that had transformed him from a modest rancher's son to a millionaire and CEO of his own self-named corporation at the age of thirty-five.

Kicking away from the desk, he smoothed a hand over his tie and once again rounded his desk.

"By all means," he told her, waving toward one of the chairs on either side of her body, which she was holding nearly as still and rigid as a statue, "have a seat and we'll talk. Like adults. About business."

For a moment she didn't move, almost as though she expected his offer to be some sort of trap. Then her muscles began to relax and she took a sideways step to her left, perching on the edge of the chair that didn't hold her little red handbag.

Knees together, spine straight, she held her folded hands on her lap, looking every inch the debutante she'd been raised to be.

The image wasn't a pleasant one for Chase. It reminded him too sharply of the girl she'd been at fourteen. The same girl who'd bruised his heart and trampled all over it with the sharp little heels of her open-toed shoes.

Pushing aside those old hurts and the feelings they evoked, he met her eyes and tried to regard her just as he would any other business associate.

"All right," he said, leaning his forearms on the top of his desk, "I'm listening. What is it you need to speak with me about?"

"You're trying to buy out my father's—my family's—company, Sanchez Restaurant Supply," she said.

"I'm *going* to buy out your father's company," he corrected.

To her credit, his comment didn't upset her or cause her to back down.

"I'm here to ask you to reconsider your decision," she

continued without flinching. "Or at the very least, to give my father a bit more time to come up with the money and resources necessary to save SRS."

"Does he think he can do that?" Chase asked, always interested in any new information that might help him get the upper hand or finalize a deal. "Come up with the financial backing, I mean."

"Yes."

She glanced away for just a split second, telling him she wasn't as confident as she was pretending to be.

"He thinks, given enough time, that he could get the company up and running successfully again. And I'm here to ask you to give him the time he needs because I'm worried about what will become of him if he loses SRS."

Her green eyes, surrounded by full black lashes that matched her long, flowing black hair, met his, wordlessly begging for his understanding and compassion.

Something warm began to unfurl low in his belly, but he clamped his jaw on his fist, and bit down on it. He'd been roped in by her soft eyes and sultry features before, and gotten kicked in the teeth for his trouble. He wouldn't let her lull him again.

"The company is his life," Elena went on. "He built it from the ground up, when he had nothing. It's the cornerstone of our family. After my mother died, he let things slide—he knows that—but he's trying now to set things right and get SRS back to where it belongs."

It was a pretty story, one no doubt designed to pull at his heartstrings. Little did she know he didn't have any heartstrings.

"What does that have to do with me?" he asked bluntly.

Those green eyes flashed for a brief moment before she seemed to remember he held her life and future—or at the very least, her father's—in his hands.

"You want to buy Sanchez Restaurant Supply and break it into pieces, selling it off to the highest bidder. I realize it would make a tidy profit for you, but I'm asking you to consider the blood, sweat and tears that went into building SRS. Consider the emotional impact losing the company will have on a good man and his family."

"Emotions have no place in business. Buying out SRS is a sound financial decision, and you're right—I stand to make a tidy sum on the deal. I can't worry about how the previous owner is going to feel about the takeover or what he did to put the company at risk to begin with."

Chase waited for that hint of fire to burn in her eyes once again, but it never came. Instead, she inclined her head once, slowly, before making one last, desperate pitch.

"I thought that's what you would say. I even understand your position. But will a few more weeks really hurt you? There have to be other companies out there that can net you just as much profit. Can't you give my father just a few more weeks, maybe a month, to see if there's something he can do to save the business? If he can't, all you've lost is a little time." She paused for a beat, looking him straight in the eye and lifting both brows. "Unless there's some *personal* reason you would be averse to helping me or my family."

She put just enough emphasis on the remark to let him know she remembered that night twenty years ago as well as he did, although he doubted her reaction was anything close to his own. He felt a spiral of shame and embarrassment begin low in his gut and he tamped it down, refusing to be controlled by memories…childhood ones, at that.

Elena Sanchez hadn't changed a bit since he'd last seen her. Oh, she'd grown into a beautiful, breathtaking woman, but then, she'd been a pretty girl.

Where it really counted, though, she was exactly the same. She still expected her feminine wiles and her family's wealth and reputation to get her whatever she desired.

Sanchez Restaurant Supply was apparently in enough trouble for her to feel compelled to try to help her father, instead of her usual attitude of letting daddy solve *her* problems. It was obvious she expected Chase to see the situation from her perspective and be mesmerized enough by the bit of skin she was flashing below the hem of her skirt and between the vee of her blouse to give her what she wanted.

Too bad for her that Chase Ramsey was not a man to be led around by the nose…or any other part of his anatomy.

"I told you," he said, with very little warmth to his words, "even if I had feelings about your family one way or the other, I wouldn't let them interfere with a business decision."

"Well, then," she said shortly, getting to her feet and retrieving her purse from the seat of the other chair, "I guess I'm wasting my time and yours. Thank you for seeing me. I'll let you get back to your work."

He watched the rigid set of her shoulders and the sensual sway of her hips as she walked away, having the uncontrollable urge to call her back.

Why should he want to keep her with him a few minutes longer, when up until today his fondest wish had been never to lay eyes on her again?

His brain was in chaos, struggling to process the conflicting feelings, while at the same time, he was kicking himself for still finding her even moderately attractive. He was like a man with split personalities: a part of him wanted to help her and part of him wanted to punish her.

"Wait," he called out, just as her long, red-tipped fingers curled around the knob of his office door.

Slowly, with obvious reluctance, she turned to face him.

"I've got a proposition for you," he told her, pushing away from his desk and moving closer, stopping before his actions could be considered intimidating.

"I happen to be in need of a female companion. A beautiful woman to accompany me on business trips and to related dinners and events."

He straightened his tie and smoothed the lines of his jacket. His statement was at least half true. He might not *need* a companion, but it certainly would be convenient to have one at his disposal. He just couldn't figure out why he felt compelled to offer the position to this particular woman.

But it didn't keep him from pressing forward, even though she had yet to respond.

"If you agree to be available to me whenever I need you, I'll agree to give your father the same amount of time to do what he can to save SRS. A day, a week, a month—it's entirely up to you."

Her lips twitched, as though she was about to speak, but before she could utter a word, he held up a hand to stop her. "You should know, before making a decision, that there will be sex involved. I'll expect you to share my bed, if that's something I require."

Elena's eyes widened and she barely stopped herself

from reaching out to slap him. What kind of woman did he think she was?

"Aren't there women you can hire for that sort of thing?" she snapped. "I'm not a prostitute."

"I never said you were. I'm simply telling you what it is that I need, and what you can do to help your father save his business."

"So you're asking me to be your mistress. Where you want me to be, when you want me to be there—a living doll you can take out of its box to look pretty and satisfy your physical needs, then put back when you're finished."

He shrugged and stuffed his hands into the front pockets of his slacks, causing the sides of his suit jacket to bunch.

"That's not exactly how I would have put it, but yes. I need a mistress and you need to buy time for your father to save his company. That's the deal, take it or leave it."

"You bastard," she muttered with a breathless laugh that was anything but amused.

"Quite possibly," he said. "But you're the one who came to me. And you should consider yourself lucky I'm making you any sort of offer at all. I could have just as easily given you a firm no and sent you on your way."

She wished she could argue, but knew he was absolutely right. Coming here had been a long shot, and the fact that he was suggesting any compromise at all was a blessing.

The question was: did she have a choice?

If she turned him down, she would have to go home and watch her father lose the business he loved, the company that essentially defined her family and made their name so well-known across Texas and the surrounding states.

But becoming Chase Ramsey's mistress... Sleeping

with a virtual stranger was a difficult concept to swallow, but she was pretty sure this particular near stranger hated her with every fiber of his being. It was probably the driving force behind his proposition, since she couldn't picture him sitting across from any other woman who came to his office to discuss business and announcing that he would give her more time if she agreed to go to bed with him.

She took a deep breath, letting the fresh oxygen fill her lungs and pump through her bloodstream. Her fingertips turned numb from the death grip she had on her handbag.

"Can I have some time to think it over?" she asked, making sure to keep her voice strong and steady. "Or do you need an answer right this minute?"

Instead of responding, he pulled his hands from his pockets and returned to his desk. Still standing, he grabbed a sheet of memo paper and a pen, then leaned over to scribble a quick note. Marching back in her direction, he handed it to her.

When she glanced down, she found a date, time and the name of the local airport. Below that, he'd added the gate number for a flight to Las Vegas.

"I'll give you until Thursday. If you show up, I'll take it to mean you agree to my terms, and your father will get the chance to try to save his company. If not—" He tipped his head and raised a brow. "I'll continue with my plans to buy out SRS."

She heard the underlying threat loud and clear, and left his office with the butterflies in her stomach flapping even harder than when she'd arrived.

Two

When Elena arrived home later that evening, she was both physically and emotionally exhausted. After her fateful meeting with Chase Ramsey, she'd gone back to her office and tried, to no avail, to focus on the appointments and paperwork involved in her job as a social worker. Thankfully, she didn't have any home visits to make and could go over her notes again later, when she was feeling more herself and less…distracted, drained, overwhelmed.

All day she had heard only four words playing over and over in her head. Chase's deep, seductive voice saying, *I need a mistress.*

I need a mistress…
I need a mistress…
I need a mistress…

And what bothered her most, what sent her mind careening into confusing, dangerous territory, was that every time those words rumbled through her brain, vivid images were quick to follow.

She could picture him stripped of that expensive suit, all tanned skin and rippling, corded muscles. Hovering over her as she lay stretched across satin sheets, naked and panting for his touch.

He was an attractive man—a handsome, virile, mouth-watering man—and she was a flesh and blood woman. No one could blame her for entertaining a fantasy or two about him, especially after he'd invited her to share his bed not five hours before.

What frightened her was that, instead of being outraged as she was initially, she was now seriously considering it.

Dropping her briefcase at the base of the coatrack just inside the front door, she kicked off her shoes and gave a sigh of relief as she wiggled her toes in freedom. She didn't usually wear such high heels to work, but the red sling-backs went best with her favorite power outfit, and she'd needed all the self-confidence she could muster to make her way to Ramsey Corporation to face Chase Ramsey himself.

In her stocking feet, she padded across the highly waxed parquet floor of the wide foyer, pausing for a moment to flip through the pile of mail on the table at the base of the steps.

She'd lived in this house in Gabriel's Crossing all her life, but lately had begun to feel uncomfortable and out of place. Maybe because it wasn't so much a house as a mansion, looking like something out of *Gone with the Wind*. There were giant Ionic columns out front; a wide, curved staircase directly across from the front door leading to the second-story; and balconies at the back overlooking several acres of beautiful Texas landscape.

Her father had had it built when Sanchez Restaurant Supply first began to turn a decent profit, and Elena had long suspected the ostentatious design was in part the home her parents had always dreamed of living in, and part proof to anyone who doubted that a first-generation Mexican-American could not only do well for himself and his family, but do *extremely* well.

And until a few years ago, she'd loved it here. As a teenager, she'd considered it another status symbol to impress her friends, and she'd taken every opportunity to have sleepovers or pool parties.

Now, though, without her mother to fill the house with her own brand of love and laughter, the house felt somewhat empty and much too large.

It was time, Elena knew, to start thinking about moving out. She should have done so years ago, but first her mother had been sick, and then her father had needed her.

Her sister, Alandra, had stuck around for the same reason.

Pulling out the letters and magazines with her name on them, Elena started up the stairs and headed for her room. All she wanted was to climb out of her clothes and sink into a nice hot bubble bath. She would light a few candles, turn on some soft classical music, and maybe even pour a glass of wine to sip while she floated away and did her best to forget Chase's troubling proposition.

Halfway down the hall, Elena knew it might be awhile before she could be alone with her exhaustion and jumbled thoughts. Her sister's choice of music—loud, blaring rock and roll—vibrated through her closed bedroom door, and Elena could hear Alandra's voice singing along.

She was about to pad by, sneak into her own room a few doors down and attempt to block out the thrumming beat of drums and a bass guitar, when Alandra's door opened and she stepped out in nothing more than a pale pink chemise-style slip and black stockings.

Both women jumped slightly in surprise, then Alandra threw her arms wide and rolled her eyes in relief.

"Oh, Elena," she called over the volume of the music, which was even louder with the door open, "I'm so glad you're home. I was about to go downstairs and ask Connie what she thinks of my outfit, but I value your opinion more."

She waved a hand, inviting Elena in, as she moved across the lushly carpeted floor and turned off the stereo. The sudden silence was almost deafening, but Elena appreciated the gesture; her sister knew how much the loud music bothered her. At a lower volume, it was almost tolerable.

"I've got a dinner in an hour. We're trying to raise money for a battered women's shelter. I'm not in charge this time, thank heavens, but I still want to look good."

While Elena perched on the end of her sister's canopied princess bed, Alandra went to the closet and pulled out two dresses on padded hangers.

"Which of these do you like best?" she asked, holding one and then the other in front of her tall, slim body.

Alandra Sanchez was, quite simply, gorgeous. Olive skin, as clear and smooth as a baby's bottom, and an hourglass figure were her shining glories. But she'd also been blessed with a pair of traffic-stopping dark brown, almond-shape eyes.

Elena's only consolation to being the less attractive sister was that everyone said they looked so much alike, she knew she wasn't exactly an ugly duckling herself.

It also helped that Alandra was as beautiful on the inside as she was on the outside. There was nothing she wouldn't do for someone, and the more they needed, the more she was willing to give. Personally, financially, it didn't matter.

She attended four or five fund-raising dinners a week, just like the one she was getting ready for now, and just as many lunches. She belonged to every "good cause" organization in the state, a few across the country, and a few more internationally: battered women and kids, underprivileged children, life-saving medical research, save the whales, save the wild mustangs, save shelter cats and dogs from euthanasia.

Alandra's greatest talent was in convincing others to give both time and money to her many worthy causes. Just being around her seemed to make everyone else care more—and sometimes feel the slightest bit guilty for not feeling so before she cornered them.

One side of Elena's mouth curved with pride. Her little sister could charm the scales off a snake and have the naked reptile thanking her afterward.

"This one?" Alandra asked, breaking into Elena's thoughts and holding up a sleek black tube dress for her perusal. Then she switched hands and held up one in pale pink with black trim, reminiscent of the Jackie O era.

In the black one, Alandra would be a knockout. Men would be drooling and falling at her feet. In the pink one, she'd still get more than her fair share of male attention, but those men would at least stand a chance of paying attention to the dinner speakers and getting interested in the cause.

"The pink one," Elena said. "Definitely."

Alandra nodded and stuck the black sheath back in the closet. "That's what I thought, but I needed a second opinion. I'll save the black one for next week when I need to raise funds for the no-kill animal shelter."

She grinned, telling Elena she was well aware of the devastating effect she would have in the other dress.

With a sigh, Elena pushed to her feet, planning to head to her own room while her sister finished getting dressed.

"Elena, wait."

She turned to find Alandra with her arms in the air, her head only half peeking through the neck of the pink and black dress. The tops of her thighs were visible, showing old-fashioned stockings held up by a sexy black garter belt.

Her sister gave a little shimmy and the dress slipped the rest of the way down. She sauntered over, turned her back to Elena, and held up the long fall of her straight black hair.

"Zip me up, and then we'll talk about what's bothering you."

Elena pulled the zipper up. "Nothing's bothering me. I'm just tired."

Alandra shook her head. "*Uh-uh.* That might work on Pop, but it won't work on me. I'm your sister; I can read you like a book."

She spun around and dragged Elena back to the bed, taking a minute to slip her feet into high-heeled black pumps before crossing her legs and perching beside her.

"All right, spill," Alandra said, sounding entirely too

chipper for the headache that was beginning to throb at Elena's temples.

"Did you do it?" she asked, lowering her voice a fraction. "Did you talk to Chase Ramsey?"

From the moment she'd first thought of going to the CEO of the Ramsey Corporation for help in saving her father's business, Elena had confided her plan to her sister. They had been best friends and confidantes since childhood, and shared just about everything with each other. Elena trusted Alandra not only to keep her secrets, but to act as a sounding board to let her know if her ideas were logical or bordering on insane.

And while Alandra had agreed that speaking with Chase Ramsey was a good idea, neither of them had breathed a word of their intentions to Victor Sanchez. Their father was a proud man and wouldn't appreciate anyone—least of all his daughters—interfering in his business or coming to his rescue.

They would only tell him, they decided, if things worked out to their benefit. Otherwise, he need never know what Elena had done.

Elena nodded, her mind flashing back to every tense, *in*tense minute of her meeting with Chase.

Alandra's eyes glittered with interest. "And how did it go? Is he going to help us?"

"That depends."

"On what?"

Elena met her sister's gaze and murmured in a voice lacking all emotion, "On whether I sleep with him."

Her sister's screech of outrage was comforting, but Elena quickly hushed her for fear their conversation would be overheard. She didn't think Pop was home yet, but Connie, their longtime housekeeper, could often be found in the hallways dusting or doing other chores.

Once Alandra had calmed down, Elena filled her in on the details of her face-to-face with Chase Ramsey, recounting every word and facial expression from the time she entered his office.

"And then he told me that he'd give Pop extra time to try to save SRS if I agreed to be his mistress. He wants me to meet him at the airport for a trip to Vegas if I'm willing to go through with it."

From her jacket pocket she pulled the slip of paper Chase had given her, and handed it to her sister. Alandra studied the scrawl before refolding the note and giving it back.

"What are you going to do?" she asked.

"I don't know." Elena released a pent-up breath and shook her head, still racked with indecision.

"Do you want me to do it?"

Elena gave a bark of laughter, then caught the flat look in her sister's eyes.

"Are you serious?" she asked. "You'd do that for me?"

Alandra shrugged. "For you, for Pop, for the family business. It wouldn't be that much of a hardship. You did say he was cute, right?"

She hadn't, and "cute" wasn't even close to the word she would use to describe Chase Ramsey's strong features, fathomless blue eyes and attractive physique.

"It's not like I have that much going on in the boudoir these days, anyway," Alandra continued with a small eye roll when Elena didn't respond. "And if this guy just wants to get laid, then he probably won't care which sister he's with."

Elena laughed again, this time in amusement. She threw her arms around Alandra and hugged her tight. "Oh, Alandra, I love you."

"I love you, too. And I'm more than willing to take this bullet for you, if you want me to."

Elena could just imagine that. The only problem was that when she pictured her sister in bed with Chase instead of herself, she felt a stab of inexplicable jealousy.

How could that be? How could she be jealous of her own sister, who was willing to sleep with a complete stranger just to save Elena and the family business? And how could she suddenly feel territorial about a man who had made her such a disrespectful offer? Primarily, she suspected, as an act of revenge for what she'd done to him as a teenager.

"No," she said, drawing a deep, cleansing breath. "I'm the one who came up with the idea of going to him in the first place. And I'm the one with a past relationship with him."

"All right," Alandra acquiesced, "then how do *you* feel about Ramsey's offer?"

Her stomach jumped at the question, followed by a peculiar, almost traitorous warmth that spread through her breasts and between her legs.

Lord, could she actually be attracted to Chase? On more than simply the detached level of a woman catching a glimpse of a good-looking man.

Could the attraction go deeper? Could she actually be considering saying yes to his proposition? To becoming his mistress?

A skittering of nerves joined the heat flowing through her bloodstream. She'd never been a man's mistress before, never been in a relationship based solely on sex. She'd dated a good number of men, and even slept with a few of them, but those relationships had always moved slowly and been based on other things, like friendship, mutual attraction, similar occupational interests.

Chase had no interest in getting to know her, and she doubted they had a single thing in common other than her father's company. He wanted her for two reasons only— to look good on his arm at business gatherings and to satisfy him in bed.

And darned if that idea wasn't becoming more appealing by the minute.

Squeezing Alandra's fingers, she felt tears prickle at the back of her eyes as she met her sister's gaze. "Is it terrible that I'm thinking of going through with it? And not entirely to help out Pop?"

Alandra gave a soft chuckle, pushing a strand of hair back from Elena's face and tucking it behind her ear. "Of course not. You're allowed to think a guy is hot and want to roll around with him for a while, with or without ulterior motives. I'd be more worried if you thought Chase Ramsey was a dog, but were still willing to sacrifice yourself and your body for SRS. The important question, I think, is how you'll feel about yourself afterward. Can you chalk it up to one of life's many adventures while remaining emotionally detached, or are you going to feel guilty or ashamed when it's all over?"

Her sister was right, but Elena knew she wasn't going to make a decision tonight. She had a couple of days before Chase left for Las Vegas, and she was going to take every one of them to make up her mind.

* * *

Chase wished he could say he was unconcerned and uninterested in whether Elena Sanchez showed up today. But in truth, he'd gotten to the airport an hour earlier than he normally would, just in case.

He'd positioned himself in one of the chairs facing the main area of the airport so he could see everyone who passed by and watch for her.

Just in case.

He'd dug out his laptop and was trying to work, making sure he had a clear view over the top of the monitor.

Just in case.

Part of him hoped she wouldn't take him up on his offer. It had been a totally spontaneous, reckless suggestion, and he still wasn't sure why he'd made it.

Maybe because he'd always wanted the chance to knock her down a few pegs. Maybe because it had been obvious that day in his office that she wasn't quite the high and mighty princess she'd been in high school, with a father wealthy enough to buy and sell Chase's own modest, hard working family and every acre of land they possessed.

Or maybe because, despite his better judgment and the gut instincts that screamed for him to back away, keep his distance and not get sucked in again by her sparkling emerald eyes, he wanted her on a purely primal, carnal level.

He'd spent the last few days kicking himself for letting his libido run rampant and make decisions for him. He wasn't a randy youth anymore, and was more than capable of ignoring and overriding his lust.

Unfortunately, all that had seemed to fly out the

window after one glimpse of her long black hair, olive skin and full, kissable lips. The shape of her breasts and flared hips in that tight red suit hadn't hurt, either.

Just the memory of her slim figure and musky perfume caused his body to stir. He shifted restlessly on the uncomfortable airport seat and tried to focus once again on the spreadsheet on the monitor in front of him.

A second later, something tall and green entered his peripheral vision. He glanced up to find Elena standing before him, and his heart skipped a beat. In surprise and sexual longing, he was sure. Not for any other reason.

Reaching out with one hand, he slowly lowered the lid of the laptop and set the computer aside, then took a minute to soak up her appearance.

She wore forest green dress pants and a blouse that matched her eyes, with a narrow slit down the front and brightly colored sequins and beads on either side as decoration. Her hair was pulled up at the sides and held in place with matching copper combs. Dangling earrings made of copper, gold and silver circles glittered at her ears. And on her feet were a pair of tan heels that looked somewhat out of place for travel and added to her height a couple of inches that she didn't need to showcase her other more-than-adequate attributes. In her hand, she held the straps of a matching handbag and at her feet was a somewhat lumpy, overstuffed carry-on bag.

Making a concerted effort not to swallow past the lump of longing in his throat, he offered a small smile and patted the seat of the empty chair to his left.

"You came. I have to say, I'm surprised."

"You didn't give me much choice. It was either this or

watch my father lose his business, with no chance of at least trying to rescue it from certain doom."

Although her little speech was dramatic and heartfelt, he refused to feel so much as a niggling of guilt. She was a big girl, capable of making her own decisions.

It was true that he'd backed her into a corner with his unusual bargain, but it was also true that anyone else would have been sent from his office with a firm and absolute no. He didn't negotiate outside of the boardroom, and even there it often wasn't necessary since he did his homework and knew how to get exactly what he wanted with a minimum of fuss and muss.

"Well, consider your sacrifice a worthwhile one." Retrieving his cell phone from one of the outside pockets of his soft leather expandable briefcase, he flipped open the top and hit the speed dial number for his office.

"Nancy," he said when his personal assistant picked up on the other end. "Do me a favor and put a hold on everything pertaining to the Sanchez Restaurant Supply takeover. I want to give the deal a bit more thought before we go any further. Thanks," he said after her affirmative response, and hung up.

"There you go," he told Elena, shifting to face her more fully and drape his arm along the back of her chair. "Whatever your father thinks he can do to pull his company out of its downward spiral, now he has the time to do it." Reaching into his jacket, he pulled out two first-class tickets to Las Vegas and held out hers.

She took it and studied her name printed in bold black ink at the top.

"You must have been pretty confident that I'd show up to buy me a ticket."

He shrugged and cocked his head to one side. "It was a calculated risk. I couldn't very well have you show up and *not* have a ticket for you, now could I? But I did make sure it was transferable, so if you hadn't shown, I could have used it for another trip later."

For the first time since she'd arrived, a ghost of a smile started to steal across her face. She raised green eyes to his, a twinkle of amusement playing behind her long, dark lashes.

"You're a very cocky man," she told him, her voice haughty but with a hint of warmth that hadn't been there earlier or in their previous meeting. "Are you ever *not* completely sure of yourself?"

Only when Elena Sanchez is in the room, he thought sourly. She was the only person who still had the ability to make him feel gawky and gangly and sixteen years old.

He would work that out of his system this week, though. Or die trying.

But aloud, for her benefit, he said, "Nope. It's been a long time since junior high," he added pointedly.

He knew his comment had hit home when her lips turned down in a frown and she glanced away.

"Yes," she said simply. "It has."

Several beats passed in uncomfortable silence before Chase let out a huff of breath and decided he probably shouldn't have needled the woman he hoped to seduce shortly after touching down in Las Vegas.

He didn't fool himself into believing her agreement to sleep with him was a done deal. Yes, she was here, which he assumed meant she had every intention of sharing his bed. But if she changed her mind at the last minute or got cold feet, he wasn't going to force her. He'd never forced any woman, and he wasn't going to start with Elena Sanchez.

Of course, she didn't know that. As far as she was concerned, flying to Las Vegas constituted her first act as his mistress, and he planned to go with that for as long as he could, hoping everything worked out just as he'd been fantasizing since she'd walked into—and out of—his office.

"Relax, Elena." He touched her arm with his free hand and rubbed the bare flesh with the side of his thumb. "We have the whole week to get to know each other better. And I promise not to jump your bones until after we've checked into the hotel."

Three

The short flight to Nevada was comfortable in first class, and quite uneventful. Chase kept his word, barely touching her the entire time and keeping their conversation to benign, unimportant topics.

But that didn't keep the nerves from skittering up and down her spine. In fact, the closer they got to the hotel, the worse her anxiety became.

He'd said he wouldn't "jump her" until after they arrived at the hotel. Did that mean the minute they hit the lobby? Would he accost her in the elevator, or as soon as they were inside the room?

She knew she was being irrational. In all the time she'd spent with Chase so far, she hadn't seen him do anything the least bit impulsive. For some reason, she simply couldn't picture him being so overcome with lust that he'd corner her in the hallway or participate in some passionate public display of affection. He was entirely too somber, too controlled.

Not that any of that kept her mind from wandering down a dozen confusing, carnal alleyways. Her body felt like a tightly strung bow, waiting for the moment he would touch her, kiss her, demand she fulfill their bargain between the sheets.

And she cursed herself for the anticipation building like a tornado at her center. For wanting him to do just that when she should be despising him for forcing her into an unacceptable situation.

A spacious black town car met them at the airport and took them directly to their hotel. The Wynn was one of the luxury hotels directly on The Strip, with marble floors, chandeliers and lots of gold and dark, polished wood. There was a casino off to the side, but it was obvious this particular establishment was meant for wealthier visitors to the city, rather than those who might come in for a weekend of fun and debauchery.

Little did the owners of the hotel know that their rich patrons could be just as interested in debauchery as those with limited funds; they were simply better at hiding their true intentions.

A bellman dressed in a maroon uniform trimmed with gold accompanied Chase and Elena to their suite. He opened the door, ushered them inside, then transferred their luggage from the wheeled cart to the bedroom.

The suite was made up of a large sitting area, a kitchenette, bathroom, and through a wide double doorway, the bedroom and a second, more private bath.

Elena had grown up with money and stayed in her fair share of luxury hotels, but even she found the opulence of this particular suite to be somewhat overwhelming.

A king-size bed filled the center of the bedroom, surrounded by ornately carved dressers and a wall of mirrors that hid the long closet space. The bathroom had a shower stall and a separate, deep Jacuzzi, both big enough, she thought, to hold three or four people.

She was standing in the doorway, admiring the almost spa-quality equipment, when Chase came up behind her and whispered in her ear.

"We have more than an hour before we need to be downstairs for dinner. Would you like to take a nap, or unpack, or…something else?"

Although he wasn't touching her at all, his voice poured over her like warm honey, his hinted suggestion sending off fireworks low in her belly. Her breathing grew choppy and she had to blink several times to stave off the sudden bout of lightheadedness that assailed her.

She wasn't ready. Not yet. She knew the moment would come when she couldn't put it off any longer, but for now he'd given her other options, and she grabbed at them like a drowning victim reaching for a life raft.

"I think we should unpack," she said a bit too loudly and a bit too brightly, spinning on her heel and slipping past him before he could protest or—worse—try to stop her.

Not waiting for a reply, she hurried to where their bags had been left and hoisted her suitcase onto the mattress. There was a luggage rack off to the side, but she decided that if the bed was covered with clothes and such, it couldn't be used for…other things.

Without a word, Chase joined her and they unpacked in silence, filling the drawers and closets, and cluttering the counter around the bathroom sinks.

When they were finished, Chase suggested they start getting ready for dinner and politely left her alone to change. She hurried with her hair and makeup, and shrugged into one of the half dozen cocktail dresses she'd brought along, knowing Chase would need time in the bedroom and bathroom to get ready himself.

Stepping into the sitting area, she found Chase standing at the bank of tall windows, staring out at the bright lights and bustling activity that made up the heart of Sin City. Though the thick, lush carpeting absorbed the sound of her footsteps, he seemed to sense her presence and turned as she rounded the end of the floral-patterned sofa.

His eyes softened when he saw her, and a gentle smile curved his lips as he skimmed her appearance, from the upswept knot of hair that left her neck and shoulders visible, to the strapless royal blue dress with its lace overlay that hugged her every curve and left her legs seductively bare. She shifted slightly and toyed with the sapphire pendant at her throat, uncomfortable with his thorough perusal.

He strode forward, taking his time and keeping his gaze firmly locked with her own.

"Nice," he murmured as he passed, careful to leave just enough space between their bodies that her skin prickled in awareness, but they never actually touched.

"I won't be long," he added before disappearing into the bedroom and closing the connecting door behind him.

* * *

Dinner, Elena was relieved to admit, passed much more enjoyably and with a lot less stress than expected. Chase had introduced her to his business associates by name, with no further explanation, rather than referring to her as his girlfriend or mistress or some other label she'd been concerned he might use. And though she'd made small talk with the other women at the table, she mostly remained silent and allowed Chase to conduct his business.

He even asked her to dance at one point, and held her close while the orchestra played a slow, romantic song. After a couple glasses of wine and the lulling atmosphere seeping into her bones, she let herself lean against the strong wall of his chest and absorb the heat of his fingers where they rested at the small of her back.

She hadn't forgotten their agreement or her reason for being here—both to help her father and become Chase's lover—but since the outcome of her decision was inevitable, she started to relax and live for the moment rather than obsess over what might come next.

They said goodnight to the others and made their way through the lobby to the bank of elevators, their footsteps slow, her arm wrapped around his and their hips brushing.

"You were great tonight," Chase said as they stepped into the empty elevator car. "Finklestein and Rogers loved you. And I think their wives were glad to have another woman at the table. My unattached state usually causes them to spend the entire meal going through a list of single young ladies they think might suit me."

Elena offered a small smile, but didn't reply.

"Bringing you along was definitely one of my better ideas."

When the elevator stopped at their floor, he led her to the suite, opened the door with his keycard and waved her inside ahead of him.

They'd left a lamp on at the far side of the room, so the suite was bathed in pale yellow light. The closed curtains kept the neon sparkle of The Strip from intruding.

"Would you like something to drink?"

Elena turned to find Chase standing near the entrance to the kitchenette, but shook her head. "I already had too much wine with dinner. Any more and I'll probably pass out and sleep for a week."

"We can't have that," he replied, his voice a low rumble.

Moving closer, he stroked the pads of his fingers down her bare arm, raising goose bumps all along her skin. His gaze held hers and she swallowed hard to keep from shivering.

When he reached her wrist, he unhooked her gold and diamond watch, setting it aside on the kitchenette counter. From the next wrist, he loosened her dangle bracelet, then slipped the rings off her fingers, adding them to the growing pile. Next came her earrings and necklace, until she stood free of accessories.

"Did I tell you how beautiful you look tonight?"

To her great embarrassment, the only reply she could manage when she opened her mouth was a strangled sort of sound. Chase grinned, his blue eyes turning storm gray and twinkling devilishly.

His hands lifted to her hair and slowly, one by one, he removed the pins holding the long locks in place. When he was finished, he drove his fingers into the twisted strands and combed them down to hang to her waist. A second later, she felt him tugging at the zipper of her dress, and then the fabric slipped from her body.

She didn't fight it, didn't grab for the garment before it hit the floor. She simply stood there and let him strip her down to her bra and panties, garter belt, stockings and high heeled shoes.

He took a small step back, just a millimeter to allow him to look his fill. "Lovely."

"They were my sister's idea." The words popped out without conscious thought and she was rewarded for her senseless muttering by his warm, lopsided smile.

"What was?"

"The garter and stockings. She told me they were sexier than pantyhose, and that you'd appreciate the difference."

His grin widened and turned even more wicked, his gaze locked on the lace edging at the tops of her thighs and the thin straps holding them up. "Your sister was right. Remind me to send her a thank-you note when we get back. And maybe a box of chocolates or some flowers."

Elena nodded absently, her insides going both weak and hot at the same time.

With one hand on her hip, the other trailing up and down the length of her arm, Chase leaned in and blew on the shell of her ear.

"Tell me, Elena," he whispered, sending shockwaves through her system, "will you come to bed with me? Now? Tonight?"

Her eyes drifted closed, the lids too heavy to keep open. Her blood felt like syrup slogging slowly through her veins.

If she'd known he was going to have this effect on her,

she probably wouldn't have come. He was too handsome, too charming and obviously had too much power over her. The power to make her weak in the knees and cloud her senses. The power to make her not only willing to sleep with a man she barely knew, but be on the verge of begging for his touch.

He had to know she was putty in his hands, had to know she was his for the taking. And yet he'd asked permission to make love to her, and was still waiting for her answer.

As much as she'd agonized over her decision to come here with him, the decision to go through with sharing his bed was easy. She wanted him, and regardless of his reasons for wanting her, there was only one response she could give.

Her lashes fluttered, and she opened her eyes to see him watching her closely, his expression intense and strained.

"Yes," she said finally.

She felt the tension seep from his body, saw the lines in his face vanish. Then, before she could form another thought, he scooped her into his arms, his long strides eating up the distance to the bedroom.

Once inside, he laid her gently on the made bed, then stepped back to divest himself of clothing. Raising up on her elbows, she watched him kick off his shoes, undo his cuff links, shed his jacket, tie, shirt and slacks. He came back to her in all his naked glory, so magnificent he made her mouth go dry.

Sitting on the edge of the bed, he opened a drawer in the nightstand and removed a box of condoms, setting them on one of the pillows in easy reach. And then he turned his attention back to her, undivided, focused. The need swirling in her belly began to build and spread outward.

He traced the line of pale flesh above the scalloped cup of her black bra, never taking his eyes from hers. Leaning in, he used his teeth to nibble and bite at her bottom lip. She opened to him, wanting more, wanting everything. And he gave it to her, covering her mouth, molding their bodies together, kissing her until she was limp and gasping for air.

When they parted, Chase grabbed her by the waist and dragged her more to the center of the bed. Then he sat back and lifted her leg until the sole of her satin pump rested flat against his bare chest.

He reached past her bent knee, letting his callused palms run up and down her thigh. His fingers caught one of the garter fasteners and deftly released it. The strap, once pulled taut, snapped back, stinging the delicate flesh of her abdomen. She gave a gasp of surprise and Chase chuckled, covering the spot with his thumb and rubbing gently.

"Sorry. I'm not used to garter belts. I'll be more careful next time."

Proving he was as good as his word, he reached around to the second clip and carefully unhooked it from the stocking.

When he began to roll the silky material down, Elena almost wished he'd snapped her again. The tiny, biting pain had to be better than the slow agony he was creating now, the heaving, writhing lust monster coming to life in her belly and between her legs. It had fangs and claws and was tearing at her insides, making her shiver and moan.

And she could tell by the simmering, possessive look in his eyes that he knew exactly what he was doing to her.

"Patience," he murmured, slipping off her shoe and the

rumpled stocking, and pressing a kiss to the inside of her bare ankle.

She made a sound deep in her throat, a cross between annoyance and a whimper. Which only seemed to amuse him all the more.

He switched to her other leg, following the same process, causing perspiration to break out along her upper lip, inside her elbows, behind her knees. When he finished, he took hold of her panties and the garter belt in both fists and slid them over her hips, down the length of her legs, and off, tossing them to the floor. Next, he reached behind her and deftly undid her bra, pitching the strapless garment in the same direction as her other lingerie.

"Now, that's what I'm talking about," Chase said, sitting back to admire his handiwork.

She fought the urge to hide her nudity with her hands or reach for a corner of the bedspread, reminding herself that she'd chosen this.

And Chase Ramsey wasn't exactly the first man to see her naked. He was merely the first in a while—as well as the most handsome and masterful.

She couldn't remember another man ever making her want him with just one look, ever making her mouth water or her body vibrate so strongly with unleashed desire.

If he was doing this to get back at her for what she'd done to him in high school, then more power to him. She felt like throwing out her arms and screaming, "Take me. Use me. Make me pay." His form of revenge was her idea of pure ecstasy.

He moved to cover her body with his own, taking her mouth in a slow, bone-melting kiss. His broad chest, with its sprinkling of dark, springy hair, flattened her breasts and rubbed against her nipples. His erection, hard and hot, nudged her stomach.

Digging her nails into his slick shoulders and back, she tipped her hips, trying to get closer, urging him to slip inside, where she needed him most.

But his exercise in torture wasn't over yet. He finished with her mouth, trailing his lips along her chin, down the column of her throat, across her collarbone and the swell of her right breast.

His tongue swept across the beaded peak and she groaned, arching upward. He continued to lick, nip, suckle and drive all sensible thought from her head.

She dug her fingers into his hair, trying to tug him away even as her back bowed into his magician's touch. A whimper slipped past her lips, and she fully expected to expire on the spot. If she survived long enough to regain the use of her limbs and brain cells, she fully intended to exact a bit of her own sweet revenge.

He lifted his head and a cocky, satisfied grin spread across his face. But the smoldering heat in his eyes belied the lighter lift of his lips.

"I want to do more," he said in a tight, gravelly voice, holding her gaze. "I want to kiss you from head to toe. Taste every inch of your skin, then come back for seconds."

He crawled up a few inches until their eyes and mouths and naughty parts aligned. Threading one hand through the hair at her temple, he reached past her and grabbed the box of condoms, struggling to open it one-handed.

"I want to," he repeated, "but I can't. I don't have that much self-control."

When he had a single square packet free, he tore the end off with his teeth and spat the plastic aside. It took him less than a second to sheath himself and settle more fully between her legs, which she had wrapped loosely around his hips.

He took her mouth, speaking between wet, breath-stealing kisses. "Later, all right? I'll lick you all over later. I promise."

With one smooth, powerful motion, he was inside her, stretching her, filling her, setting her nerve endings on fire. Air hissed through his clenched teeth as he held himself perfectly still above her, the muscles in his throat roped and taut.

She knew he was waiting for her, giving her time to adjust to his invasion, the size and hardness of his impressive length.

But she didn't need time. She only needed him.

From the moment he'd entered her, everything about this encounter had felt right. And now all she wanted was for him to move, to fill her even more fully and send her flying over the abyss that hovered just out of reach.

Twining her arms around his neck to match the twist of her legs at his hips, she drew him closer. "Don't stop now," she whispered a split second before their mouths met.

He groaned, the sound vibrating against her lips, through her torso and limbs and into her soul.

His hands tightened on her waist, lifting her slightly as he pulled back. She started to whimper at the friction he created and the sudden loss of his heat, but before the noise could work its way up from her diaphragm, he thrust forward again.

Slowly, methodically, he moved in and out. Smooth motions at first, then building in speed and intensity.

Her breathing increased, her lungs contracting to absorb less and less oxygen with each breath. She raised her legs higher, gripping him about the waist, doing everything she could to pull him deeper.

It wasn't enough. He was pounding into her now, his fingers digging into the flesh of her buttocks, but still she wanted more. She wanted harder, faster, stronger… *More, more, more.*

Even as she thought it, the words tumbled from her lips. Broken and disjointed, but directly into Chase's ear.

He heard, agreed, obeyed, taking her higher and faster until she was gasping. Her body strained for him, strained for release.

And then it hit with the impact of a bullet, making her cry out and claw at his back with her nails. Her inner muscles spasmed around him, and she moaned in wonder as he took her climbing again.

The second climax was as strong as the first, rocking her to her very core. And this time, he came with her, grinding his mouth to hers as he pumped one last time, then went rigid above her.

For several long minutes, they lay there, tangled and still, their ragged breathing the only sound in the otherwise silent room. Elena couldn't move, her bones weak, her will nonexistent.

She hadn't ever experienced an orgasm even close to that in her adult life, not to mention the level of sensuality, passion, eroticism and intensity he'd shown her.

If she'd ever suspected sex with Chase Ramsey would be half as satisfying as what they'd just done, she'd have been tempted to look him up long ago…or seduce him back in high school.

She might even have to thank him for blackmailing her

into this situation, because so far, being his mistress was turning out to have some incredible perks.

With a reluctant groan, he rolled aside. The air in the room washed over her naked, damp body, making her shiver. But a second later, he'd pulled back the bedspread and was dragging her toward the headboard. He tucked her under the covers, propped a pillow beneath her head and then slipped an arm around her shoulders and hugged her close.

"Go to sleep," he whispered, pressing a kiss to the side of her head.

As pillow talk went, it was somewhat lacking, but she was too tired and too satisfied to care. Curling into him, she closed her eyes and let herself drift off, only vaguely aware of the smile stretched across her face.

Four

Elena awoke the next morning to a gentle clinking and the heavenly smell of scrambled eggs and fresh-brewed coffee. She rolled to her back, inhaling deeply and stretching her arms high above her head before forcing her eyes open.

The room was still dark, the bed so soft and warm and comfortable, she never wanted to leave it. But the scent of breakfast and sounds of someone moving around in the other room drove her to throw back the covers and sit up.

It took her a moment to realize she was stark naked, the cream-colored satin sheets soft against her bare skin. And then she remembered the events of last evening, a bright flush heating her from her toes to her hairline. She couldn't decide if she was embarrassed or sorry Chase wasn't still in bed beside her so they could once again do everything they'd done last night—and more.

Padding across the soft plush carpet, she found a robe and nightie set in one of the dresser drawers and put them on, then took a few minutes to brush her teeth and wash her face before moving to the open doorway between the bedroom and sitting room.

Chase was already dressed in a charcoal-gray suit, white shirt, and seafoam tie, his black hair neatly combed and styled. He sat at the round mahogany table arranged in front of the wide open windows, sipping hot coffee and reading the morning paper.

Running her fingers through her still sleep-tousled hair, she cleared her throat and started forward.

He lifted his head when he noticed her approach and gave her a small smile. "Morning. Did you sleep well?"

She nodded, taking the seat across from him and reaching for the coffee carafe to pour herself a cup.

"I didn't know what you'd like for breakfast, so I ordered a little of everything," he told her, reaching for the room service cart a few inches away and removing the silver lids from several platters.

There were pancakes, scrambled eggs, crisp bacon and sausage links and a wide array of fresh, seasonal fruit. It looked delicious, and she wasted no time filling her plate. She added cream and sugar to her coffee and poured a bit of syrup over her pancakes before digging in.

A second later, she lifted her head and glanced at Chase. "Aren't you eating?" she asked.

He shook his head and lifted his cup to his lips. "Coffee's all I need in the morning."

Having him watch her eat what amounted to a truckload of food while he merely sipped his black coffee made her feel like a glutton. Not that it would stop her, she thought, popping a bite of honeydew melon in her mouth.

After she swallowed, she waved her fork at him, distracting him once again from the business section of the *Las Vegas Review-Journal.*

"It's not healthy to skip breakfast, you know," she told him, breaking a slice of bacon into smaller pieces and nibbling them one at a time. "It's the most important meal of the day."

One side of his mouth lifted indulgently before he returned his attention to the paper without a word.

She ate in silence awhile longer, enjoying the sunny view out the bank of tall windows, but not her current company. Finally, she put down her fork and grabbed a second plate, filling it with small portions of the same items on her own.

"Here," she said, pushing the paper aside with a rattle and placing the plate in front of him. "You're driving me crazy. You have to eat something."

He stared at her for a long minute, brows knit in a frown. "I don't need anything to eat."

He started to open his paper again and straighten the page she'd wrinkled. With a sigh, she half-stood and took the paper from his hands. Before he could grab it back, she returned to her seat and leaned far enough away that he couldn't reach her unless he got up and came around the table.

"How about if I read the paper to you while you eat?" she offered brightly.

His frown turned into a full-blown scowl. "Elena," he murmured, lacing her name with dire warning. "I didn't bring you along to mother me or tell me what to do. I'm thirty-five years old and already set in my ways. I have a routine and I like to stick to it. Now give me back my paper."

She tipped her head. "Indulge me. Please? You've got a busy day ahead of you, and we expended quite a bit of energy last night. You need to keep your strength up or you'll be of absolutely no use to me in bed tonight."

She felt her cheeks heat at her own audacity, but forced herself not to squirm under his intense regard. He studied her for several long seconds while her insides turned to jelly.

And then he let out a bark of laughter and picked up his fork.

"Fine," he said. "You read, I'll eat. And don't worry," he added with a pointed, just-shy-of-boiling glance, "I'll have plenty of energy for anything you might have in mind tonight."

Opening the paper to hide any more bright color that might suffuse her face, she swallowed hard and began reading where she thought he'd left off. The information was boring enough to counteract the caffeine already coursing through her bloodstream, but she didn't stop until she'd reached the last page. She even recapped the comics for him one by one.

When she was finished, she folded the paper and set it aside, delighted to see that he'd cleaned his plate and even poured himself a small glass of orange juice.

"I've changed my mind," he said. "From now on, I'm going to have a huge, four-course breakfast…and I'll leave the reading of the morning paper to you. Aloud, and in that amazingly sultry voice of yours."

Sultry? She'd never thought of her voice as sultry before. A little low and raspy at times, but never sultry.

"You have a touch of your father's accent, did you know that? Like a hint of Mexico just beneath the Texas twang."

Considering his own Texas drawl was as thick, if not thicker, than her own, she didn't think he had much room to talk. But still, the compliment—and she did take it as a compliment—washed over her, warming her from the inside out.

"Maybe you could read to me again tonight," he continued. "In bed. Something sexy and a little naughty."

Nerves jangled in her stomach, unexpected desire skating down her spine like an Olympic hopeful going for the gold.

"Do you have any sexy or naughty reading material?" she asked, surprised when the words came out strong and surprisingly sensual. For the first time, she heard the sultriness he'd spoken of, as well as an unspoken, almost unintentional invitation.

And from the look in his eyes, she knew he heard it, too.

"Not here," he said, his voice tight and graveled with lust. "But I'll find something by this evening even if I have to buy up every book and magazine publisher on the West Coast."

He held her gaze and it was all she could do not to wiggle in her seat, both from nerves and a growing sense of longing. How he could have such an effect on her after such a short amount of time, she didn't know. But it was there, strong and powerful and alive.

"Unfortunately," he went on, dragging his gaze away from her to check his watch, his voice returning to normal, "I have to get going or I'll be late for my first meeting."

Pushing his chair away from the table, he stood and dug out his billfold. "I'll be busy pretty much all day, so I'm afraid you'll have to find something to keep yourself occupied. Here, take these." He handed her a gold card and a stack of crisp bills in large denominations. "Go shopping, do lunch, have fun. I'll see you back here around four. We have another business dinner I'll want you to be ready for, all right?"

She took the cash and credit card, even though she didn't like it. Being handed money to "keep herself occupied" made her feel cheap, entirely too much like a paid companion. But then, she supposed that was just part of the job when one agreed to become a man's mistress.

Throwing back the last swallows of his coffee, he crossed the room for his briefcase, then headed for the door. With his hand on the knob, he tossed an already distracted "See you later" over his shoulder before disappearing into the hall.

The door clicked closed behind him, leaving Elena alone in the sprawling suite. She glanced down at the wad of bills in one hand and the credit card in the other.

Well, that had gone from interesting to disappointing in the blink of an eye, she thought. But this wasn't a vacation; it was a work week for Chase, and the fulfillment of a business agreement for her.

So she would find something to fill her day like a good mistress, and be back in time to get ready for her next dinner performance.

Where the hell was she?

Chase stood in front of the bedroom bureau, straightening his tie in the mirror for what had to be the fifth or sixth time.

He was showered, dressed and ready for the dinner meeting. The only thing missing was his date.

He glanced at his watch again, even though only a minute had passed since the last time he'd checked, and muttered a colorful oath.

She was almost an hour late. He'd told her to be back in the room by four o'clock, and here it was going on five.

She was probably busy burning up his credit card with dozens of clothes, shoes and expensive trinket purchases. What more could he expect of a spoiled, selfish debutante like Elena Sanchez?

The problem was, she hadn't acted spoiled or selfish since meeting him at the airport. He hadn't even seen any signs of the shallow girl she used to be—her bossiness at breakfast that morning notwithstanding.

He'd actually found her strong-arm tactics during that little incident amusing…followed by highly erotic when she'd agreed to use that husky, arousing voice of hers to read to him in bed.

Of course, now he knew the last day and a half was more of a fluke than anything else. He'd given her his gold card and a stack of cash in fairly large bills, and she'd apparently found a way to blow through it all. Enough so that she was still busy shopping.

Which didn't surprise him in the least. Truth be known, he'd given her such a long lead line to prove—to himself, if no one else—exactly what he knew deep down in his bones. Elena Sanchez hadn't changed. She was still indulgent, self-involved, too beautiful for her own good, and she put her own comforts and desires above the feelings or well-being of others.

The pointed reminder was worth paying a few thousand dollars to his credit card company.

But if she didn't get back soon, if she made him late for this very important business dinner, he would not only make her pay the charge bill herself, but he'd put her on the first plane back to Gabriel's Crossing and have her father's company bought out and in his portfolio by morning.

He swore again and was just turning his wrist to check his watch for the ten millionth time when he heard the door to the suite click open.

"Finally," he breathed, following that by another grumbled curse.

"Where the hell have you been?" he charged, turning on his heel and marching into the other room.

He expected to find her grinning from ear to ear, her hands full of boutique bags, her arms piled high with ribboned boxes. She'd probably want to show him everything he'd bought her, maybe model some designer dresses and sexy new lingerie.

He might even be willing to sit through a lingerie fashion show…later, after they got back from dinner and he wasn't in such a foul mood.

"Sorry," she apologized, rounding the corner of the kitchenette.

She looked rumpled and windblown, her simple, sleeveless cotton blouse and denim skirt wrinkled, her hair starting to fall out of its now-crooked ponytail. Her face and shoulders rosy from the glaring Las Vegas sun.

As far as he could see, there wasn't a single bag or box anywhere near her.

He paused in mid-step, momentarily confused.

Maybe she was having everything delivered. But just to be sure, he walked the rest of the way across the room and glanced toward the door.

Nothing.

She didn't look overly happy or bubbly or excited, either, the way most women would after what amounted to a carte blanche shopping spree.

"You're late," he pointed out, uncomfortable with the knowledge that she'd knocked him off his guard, managed to sidetrack him from his focus on her whereabouts and their dinner schedule.

"I said I was sorry," she told him, not the least intimidated by his accusatory tone or thunderous expression. "But I won't take long to get ready, I promise."

Pulling the ponytail holder from her hair, she started for the bedroom, already unbuttoning her blouse. "I'll only be twenty minutes."

She left the connecting doors open and he could hear her moving around. Shedding clothes. Opening dresser drawers and closet doors. Stepping into the bathroom, out, then in again. The bathroom door closed and he heard the shower turn on.

Regardless of what she said, he fully expected her to take at least an hour to change and do her hair and makeup. He didn't know any woman who wouldn't.

A quick glance at his watch showed that if she took an hour—an hour, and not one minute more—they could still make it down to the hotel restaurant on time. Barely, but they would make it.

Strolling into the bedroom, he moved to the dresser where he'd abandoned his cufflinks when he'd heard her come in, trying not to imagine Elena's wet, soapy, naked body in the generous shower stall. A space large enough to fit two comfortably...in any number of creative positions.

Clearing his throat, he turned his attention back to attaching the gold and diamond studs at his wrists. Just because he was annoyed at her tardiness didn't mean he didn't still want her. If they weren't already running late, he'd leave a trail of clothing behind on the walk to the bathroom and join her for a long, enjoyable steam— among other things.

Afraid that he would give in to temptation if he stayed this close to her for much longer, he turned. As it was, he ran the risk of spending the rest of the evening trying to hide an embarrassing arousal.

But before he went a step, his gaze caught on two items on the dresser top. His credit card and the pile of cash he'd handed Elena earlier.

Ignoring the card, he picked up the bills and counted them out. Only twenty-odd dollars missing, from the hundreds he'd given her.

Well, that wasn't so surprising, he decided. She'd probably charged just about everything all day. The cash could have been used solely for tips or some such.

In the bathroom, the water shut off and he quickly replaced the cash beside the card. He didn't want her to know he'd fanned through it. And since he would probably have supplied her with the same again tomorrow, he might as well leave them where she'd put them.

But just out of curiosity...

He quickly glanced at the phone number on the back of the credit card, memorizing it, then slipping quietly from the room before she emerged from the bathroom. Closing the door silently behind him, he crossed to the phone on the desk in the far corner.

It took a few minutes to get through to an operator and verify his identity, then a second more to make his request and wait for the answer. Had there been any charges on his account today, and if so, how much did it total?

He thanked the woman on the other end of the line and returned the handset to its cradle, a deep frown marring his brow and tugging his mouth down at the sides.

Zero. Zero charges. His balance was the same as it had been before, and the last purchase was one he'd made himself.

Now he was even more confused than before. She'd been gone all day, on his dime, presumably shopping, yet hadn't spent more than thirty dollars.

He didn't know any woman who could shop all day and only spend thirty bucks.

So if she hadn't been shopping, where had she been and what had she been up to?

Before he could devise a list of possibilities, the bedroom door opened and she stepped out, looking like every man's fantasy come to life. Her hair was swept up into an artful twist. Her long black gown glittered with silver in the lamplight. A slit ran from her ankles to very high on her thigh, and the front was cut low, fastening around her neck with a single strap, leaving the front of her neck, shoulders and back bare.

She wore minimal jewelry—a couple of rings, a pair of silver string earrings and a small charm on a thin silver necklace that matched the bracelet on her wrist—and three-inch spike heels that caused his blood to thicken and slog through his veins.

"Twenty minutes, as promised," she said, making a small pirouette where she stood.

The gown showed off her womanly shape as though she were naked, and he suddenly wanted to keep her inside the room with him rather than take her out, so no one else could see her.

"What do you think?"

He thought way too many things, none of them suitable for delicate ears or pre-dinner conversation. After dinner, though…that was a whole different story.

"Good. Good. You look good." His tongue felt like an old gym sock in his mouth, and even though he knew he wasn't making much sense, he was content to be able to form words at all. The synapse in his brain was barely firing, cells washing away to join all the others in his body south of the equator.

To buy a few much-needed moments to recover his senses, he cleared his throat and checked his watch. She was right; she'd only taken a little over twenty minutes to get ready, from the time she'd disappeared into the bedroom…twenty-five counting the time he'd wasted standing there feeling speechless and steamrolled.

"Okay. Well, then…" He tugged at his cuffs, straightened his tie and somehow managed to step forward, offering his arm. "Are we ready to go?"

She nodded, meeting him halfway. He noticed the shawl in her other hand and took it from her, draping the long-fringed lace around her shoulders.

"You look amazing," he said, perhaps belatedly.

"Thank you."

He pulled open the door, holding it until she'd passed into the hall, then hooked her arm around his elbow again and guided her to the elevator. Their reflection shimmered back at them in the polished golden doors, and he couldn't help noticing how good she looked standing beside him. Tall, glamorous, gorgeous.

He'd known she was beautiful when he'd suggested this arrangement—a man would have to be blind not to, and even then, any man worth his salt would have a pretty good idea of her charms just from her voice and the way she handled herself.

He'd also known she would make a good impression on his associates. She was funny and charismatic and knew when to put in a few words or hold her tongue while business was being discussed. And there was no arguing she was easy on the eyes.

What he hadn't counted on was the force of his attraction to her.

Beautiful women were nothing new to Chase Ramsey. He was wealthy, a self-made multimillionaire, which happened to be an attribute that a lot of women apparently found irresistible.

And he'd enjoyed his fair share of them. Some might say he used them, asking them out only when he needed a date for one event or another, and then taking them to bed—a place they were always more than willing to go.

But the way he saw it, any using was mutual. They wanted to be with him because he had money, wanted to be seen with him because of his power and prestige.

And most of them, whether they were blatant about it

or not, harbored hopes of finagling a wedding ring out of him and snagging themselves a rich husband.

Elena, however, was in an entirely different category.

She didn't seem impressed by his wealth at all. Yes, her family had money of their own, but so did the families of a lot of women he dated. That never kept them from wheedling for or accepting expensive gifts. Permission to use his credit card for the day would have had most of them squealing like a litter of hungry piglets.

She didn't take forever in the bathroom or fuss obsessively over her appearance, and once she was ready, she was ready. She carried herself with confidence and seemed comfortable with whatever she was wearing instead of fidgeting with every little thing.

It was that confidence, her silent assurance, that turned him on almost as much as her shapely body and passionate nature.

Aside from that, he also found her simply fascinating. She never did what he expected, never reacted to things quite the way he thought she would.

And she hadn't charged a single damn thing to his credit card, which he had to admit was driving him positively crazy. He wanted to know where she'd been all day, what she'd been up to.

He *needed* to know.

"So," he murmured as the elevator doors whooshed open and they stepped inside the plush compartment. "What did you do today?"

Five

Elena raised the back of her hand to her mouth to stifle a yawn. It had been a long day, and she was suddenly feeling every minute of it. The two Manhattans she'd sipped through dinner probably hadn't helped, either.

"Sleepy?" Chase asked, brushing a loose tendril of hair away from her face.

She offered a small smile and leaned into his touch as the same elevator that had taken them down to the lobby a few hours before now took them back up to their floor.

It was amazing how comfortable she felt with him after such a short time, and it worried her. She'd expected their relationship to be cold, businesslike. Intimate, but functional.

Instead, things between them had been warm and friendly. She liked it, and that bothered her most—that she liked it maybe a bit too much.

"I'm a little tired," she answered.

His hand slid from the lobe of her ear to the nape of her neck, where he gently kneaded the taut muscles with his calloused fingertips.

"You must have had a busy day."

It wasn't the first time he'd tried to find out how she'd spent the afternoon. But so far, she'd avoided giving him a straight answer. It wasn't that her activities were that much of a secret, just that she didn't feel like sharing.

He'd handed her a wad of cash and a credit card, and basically told her to keep herself occupied while he worked. Well, she had—without spending more than twenty-five or thirty dollars of his money, either. Since she hadn't let him foot the bill for more than a short cab ride and a salad for lunch, it was no one's business but her own how she'd stayed busy.

When it became apparent she wasn't going to answer, he went on.

"When we get back to the room, I'll help you slip out of these clothes, then turn down the covers and we'll crawl into bed."

"Just to sleep?" she teased.

"Just to sleep," he assured her. And then his lips curved and a devilish glint sparkled in his blue eyes. "Unless you're interested in something else."

A slow heat began to unfurl low in her belly. That was another thing she found surprising about this situation…that making love with him didn't feel like a chore she had to subject herself to in order to help her father save his company. She *liked* being with him, and was already looking forward to spending the night in his arms. Just the thought made warmth pour through her system and put her nerve endings on red alert.

"What did you have in mind?" she asked as the elevator doors opened and they stepped into the hallway, any drowsiness quickly morphing into arousal and anticipation.

"Oh, I don't know," he drawled, his arm twined with hers as they strolled slowly toward their suite. "We didn't have dessert with dinner so maybe we should order something sweet from room service."

They stopped in front of their door and he fitted the key card into the lock, waiting for the light to flash green.

"Strawberries and champagne?" he suggested, holding the door open for her. "I could nibble juice from your chin and trickle champagne into your navel. Or hot fudge sundaes. I understand chocolate sauce tastes even better licked off a beautiful woman's naked flesh."

If she hadn't been turned on before, the mental images he was creating certainly aroused her. She shivered as she thought of his tongue scraping along her skin, of chocolate and ice cream mixing with passion in her mouth as he kissed her after cleaning them from her body.

"So what will it be?" he asked when she was halfway across the room. "Dessert or straight to bed?"

His voice sounded farther away than she'd expected, and she turned to find him leaning against the wall, just a few steps past the closed and locked door. His arms were crossed over his chest, one leg cocked over the other at the ankle.

One glimpse of him standing there, looking so casually relaxed yet so intensely masculine, and she knew there was no way she'd be sleeping tonight. At least not anytime soon.

But that didn't mean she couldn't have a little fun with him first.

"I'd like to go straight to bed," she said, feigning a yawn that a few minutes ago would have been real. Reaching up to remove the pins from her hair, she watched the air of confidence seep from his expression, the cockiness disappear from the firm set of his stance. His reaction amused her, but she didn't tease him for long.

Shaking her head and letting the long strands of her hair fall to the middle of her back, she added, "With the strawberries, champagne *and* a hot fudge sundae. With nuts on top, please."

She turned on her heel and sashayed toward the bedroom, but not before she saw the wide, positively predatory grin that spread across his face. It wouldn't have surprised her if he'd pushed away from the wall and sprung on her like some sleek jungle beast. A part of her even wished he'd do just that.

They would fall to the floor right where she was standing in a tangle of limbs, his heavy frame pinning her down. Clothes would be torn off, tossed away or left in tatters. Mouths and hands would be everywhere. They would come together fast, hot, frantically, the carpet leaving them scraped and raw.

And it would all be worth it.

She almost whimpered at the very idea, moist heat pooling between her legs, making her weak in the knees. She bit her lip, wondering what she might do to make it happen.

But in the end, she couldn't think of anything that felt right. She wasn't used to seducing handsome men, let alone devising a plan to get one to attack her.

So she settled for simply lifting her hands to the back of her neck and unhooking the single strap of her dress. The two pieces of material fell, an arm across her breasts the only thing keeping her from being completely bare.

"You will bring everything into the bedroom when it gets here, won't you?" she asked as seductively as she could manage. Then, without waiting for an answer, she stepped into the other room and closed the door behind her.

Her heart was beating a mile a minute. She'd never done anything like that before—taunted a man, tried to work him into a lather and lure him into bed.

And now she would have to deliver. At the speed of light, she raced around the room, undressing. She kicked her shoes off so they each flew in different directions. Her dress fell to the floor and she opened the closet door to kick it inside. It was no way to treat an obscenely expensive designer gown, but at the moment she couldn't care less.

Hopping from foot to foot, she made her way to the bathroom while working to undo her garter belt and roll off her black stockings. She left them in a ball on the floor, along with her matching black panties.

Naked, she stood at the sink, in front of the huge wall-to-wall mirror, and quickly brushed her teeth, washed her face, ran a comb through her hair. She reapplied a dab of perfume behind each ear and at the pulse points of her wrists, then hurried back to the bed.

Sweeping back the covers, she leaped onto the ivory satin sheets, plumped a couple pillows behind her back and tried to adopt a sexy, alluring pose. Marilyn Monroe, Jane Russell, Anna Nicole Smith…she thought of every pinup girl she could remember and tried to channel their spirits.

She pulled the sheet up to her waist, then over her breasts, then threw it off again. Bent her legs to the left, then the right. Threw an arm over her head, then scooted down and laid spread-eagle across the bed like the smorgasbord she hoped he would use her as.

When she heard the rattle of the doorknob, she startled, swallowed a panicked squeak and froze in the best position she could come up with at the last minute. She let the muscles in her face go lax and half-closed her eyes, hoping he wouldn't notice she was a nervous wreck. She wanted him to think she'd just been lounging on the bed, waiting for him to serve her.

The bedroom door opened and he strolled in, dragging a room service cart behind him. This time it held a bowl of strawberries, a magnum of champagne on ice, two glasses and a very large, decadent, already melting ice cream sundae.

Normally, her stomach would have rumbled at such delicious-looking fare. But at the moment, it was her other four senses and her raging libido that were starving for attention.

Chase turned, his gaze soaking her in, slowly skimming from head to toe. From the hardening of his jaw and the steam rising behind his sea-blue eyes, she thought he must like what he saw.

A thrill rolled through her and she sat up straight, careful to act sleepy and nonchalant.

"Mmm," she murmured. "It looks good."

"Yes," he said slowly, still staring intently at her. "It does."

After a few tense seconds when she thought he might forget the food altogether and simply lunge at her, he picked up the bottle of Roederer Cristal, dried the bottom with a cloth napkin and popped the cork. He poured the champagne into both flutes, then handed one to her, followed by the bowl of strawberries.

She took a plump, bright red berry and bit into the tip before taking a sip of champagne.

"Good?" he asked, sampling a piece of fruit on his own.

"Delicious."

Taking a long swallow of champagne, he set his glass and the bowl of strawberries aside and began shrugging out of his clothes. Suit jacket, tie, shoes…they all evaporated as though they were made of smoke.

As naked as she, he turned back to the wheeled cart, grabbed the dripping sundae and a spoon and climbed onto the wide mattress beside her.

"*This* is what I'm hungry for," he said.

He lowered her gently until she fell back against the pillows. Before she'd even had a chance to get comfortable or wonder what he might do next, he dropped a dollop of whipped cream right in the center of her belly button.

She gave a little yelp and nearly came up off the bed, her first instinct to get the chilly substance off her bare skin. But the clicking of his tongue and the shimmering heat in his glance reminded her of the game they were playing.

Taking a deep breath, she relaxed her body and sank farther into the pillows and glossy sheets, ready to let him do what he wished with his sweet, sticky dessert and her naked, vulnerable body.

He grinned, flashing straight white teeth at her capitulation and digging once again into the sundae.

It took all of her control, all of her concentration not to squirm and shiver as he decorated her nipples, left dribbles of hot fudge sauce along her chest, midsection and inner thighs. Plucking the bright red maraschino cherry off the top by its stem, he placed it on top of the whipped cream on her navel.

"There," he announced, setting the remainder of the sundae on the nightstand and sitting back to admire his handiwork. "Perfect."

She chuckled, a brittle, throaty sound working its way up from her diaphragm. A trickle of vanilla ice cream was melting between her tightly closed legs, heading in a direction where she wanted only warmth—preferably created by Chase. "It's cold."

"Hmm," he hummed, shifting closer. "Let me see what I can do to heat things up."

His low tone and the determined look in his eyes sent a ripple of anticipation skating down her spine, taking precedence over the goose bumps breaking out along her skin.

He leaned in, covering a smear of chocolate with his tongue, then dragging upward to the underside of her breast. The action caused her nipples to bead beneath the fluffy white clouds he'd deposited there.

She writhed beneath him, her back arching, her arms lifting automatically to reach for him.

"Ah, ah, ah," he warned without moving his lips from her skin. The words vibrated through her. "No touching from you. Not yet."

His hands closed around her wrists, pushing her arms up over her head. "Lie back and enjoy."

Easier said than done, she thought. At the moment, his idea of enjoyment bordered on torment—and he was just getting started.

He licked the whipped cream crowning one breast, tiny flickers like a cat lapping at a bowl of milk, until her nipple was bare.

Elena bit down hard on her bottom lip to keep from crying out as he switched to her other breast. This time he gave a low growl and engulfed the tip all at once. No small nibbles to draw out the agony, but that didn't make the pleasure any less sharp.

Her hands clutched the pillow behind her head, her heels dug into the mattress. Already, her inner muscles were tightening, begging for release. "Chase, please."

"Soon," he whispered, kissing his way back down her stomach, picking up stray hot fudge as he went. "Very soon."

He slurped the whipped topping from her belly button, working around the cherry, leaving it to fill the indent of her navel. Sliding down, hands skimming her hips, he parted her thighs and began to nuzzle ice cream from between them.

But he didn't stop there. Even though she was sure the ice cream hadn't dripped any deeper, he lifted her legs to his shoulders and began to explore. He nibbled, licked, stroked her moist folds until she couldn't help but clutch at his hair—to pull him away or hold him close, she didn't know.

When he concentrated his efforts on the hidden bud of her desire, her blood pressure skyrocketed and she climaxed against his mouth almost without warning. Tremors racked her body and she gasped for breath, arms falling to her sides as her bones and muscles turned the consistency of watery oatmeal.

With a feral grin, Chase raised his head and lifted himself on all fours to hover over her. He started to crawl forward, pausing only long enough to close his teeth on the stem of the cherry in her navel and carry it with him to her mouth. Her lips were already parted, her lungs still straining for oxygen.

"No. No more," she panted, letting her eyes fall closed. "I can't take any more."

"Sure you can." His words were slightly muted as he talked through his teeth, still holding the cherry by its stem. "Open."

With a sigh that was part exhaustion, part reluctant anticipation, she opened her mouth and let him drop the cherry inside.

"Now close."

She did, and he tugged, breaking the stem away from the plump, sweet fruit.

"Chew," he ordered.

Maraschino cherries were one of her favorites and she gave a little moan of enjoyment as the tart juices played over her taste buds and ran down her throat.

In a much softer, huskier voice, Chase said, "Now open again."

When she did, he meshed his mouth with hers, kissing her deeply, passionately, thoroughly. To her great surprise she found her strength coming back and her arms snaking up to wrap around his shoulders.

He pulled back slightly, his lips curled up at the corners as he hummed with pleasure. "That is the best hot fudge sundae I've ever tasted. I never want to eat one with just a spoon again."

Elena gave a shuddery chuckle. She didn't know if she could live through another session like that, but she was absolutely sure she would never see sundaes in quite the same way. She would never be able to look at one without remembering this night and the wicked things Chase Ramsey could do with a bit of whipped cream, chocolate sauce and his tongue.

Oh, that tongue!

"But we aren't finished yet," he said.

Scraping his teeth along her jaw and biting her earlobe, he reached into the nightstand drawer for a condom. He tore open the packet and sheathed himself, all without taking his focus from her neck and shoulder. Settling more fully into the cradle of her thighs, he found her feminine opening and sank inside in one long, sleek movement.

She was already wet and more than ready for his entry. Only moments ago, she'd thought herself ruined for ever again experiencing an ounce of pleasure. But she'd underestimated the power of Chase's mode of persuasion.

He was ruthless, taking no prisoners. There was no slow buildup this time around, no teasing or tantalizing. He filled her to overflowing and began to pound into her like a piston.

His fingers dug into the flesh of her buttocks, pulling her closer to meet him on each thrust.

Harder, faster, he drove the air from her lungs, his own breaths coming rapidly. She tightened her legs around his waist, her nails raking his sweat-slick back.

"Chase," she moaned.

"Elena," he groaned in return before burying his face in the curve of her neck and biting gently on the taut line of muscle that ran across to her shoulder.

The orgasm, when it came, rocked her, made the room feel like it was spinning around them and spilled through her like a tidal wave. She gasped…then stopped breathing altogether. Above her, Chase gave one deep, final thrust and shouted with completion.

A second later, he collapsed, his weight pressing her into the mattress. Instead of being uncomfortable, she smiled at the boneless, total relaxation taking over his body. She could feel his heart racing in his chest, in tandem with her own, his breath stirring her hair.

Sooner than she'd have liked, he groaned and rolled away. He lay flat on his back, arms and legs spread wide, while he continued to breathe heavily.

"You'll be the death of me, Elena," he said with a heartfelt sigh, rolling his head to the side so he could look at her. He grinned. "But I'll die a happy man."

Before she could respond, he pushed up from the bed and walked stark naked to the bathroom, closing the door behind him. Suddenly conscious of her blatant nudity and the fact that she was sprawled like a rag doll in a less-than-attractive position, she hopped up and hurried to the dresser for a nightgown.

Slipping it on, she glanced at her reflection in the mirror. Her cheeks were rosy, the rest of her skin aglow. Her lips looked puffy, reminding her of that old term, "bee-stung."

She'd never had bee-stung lips before. But then, she'd never been kissed quite as senseless, quite as passionately before, either.

Since her hair was a tousled mess, she ran her fingers through to untangle the long strands, turning just as the bathroom door opened. Chase stood there, still blessedly naked, his hands braced on either side of the doorjamb. Just the sight of him made her pulse pick up and the slippery fabric of the nightie feel rough against her bare skin.

"You didn't have to get dressed on my account," he quipped.

She smiled somewhat nervously, curling her painted toes into the soft, thick carpeting. "I'm not used to lying around in the altogether."

"Too bad," he said, striding forward and stopping directly in front of her. Using the knuckle of his index finger, he tipped her head up until she had no choice but to meet his crystal blue eyes. "That's something I'd pay money to see. Besides, we weren't entirely finished with our dessert. We still have champagne and quite a few strawberries to get through."

"Well…" she said slowly, butterflies flapping sensuously in her belly, her courage growing in direct proportion to the longing heating up his gaze. Hooking her thumbs under the thin spaghetti straps at her shoulders, she slowly began to peel them down her arms. "It's just a teeny, tiny scrap of satin. You could get it off again in no time, if you really wanted to."

Desire flashed across his face, followed by the wicked lift of one dark brow. "Really?"

He replaced her thumbs with his own fingers and finished the job of sliding the top of the nightgown down, uncovering her chest, then her breasts and ribcage. As soon as the straps were free of her arms, he released them, letting the garment drop to the floor where it pooled around her feet.

"Well, will you look at that," he murmured in mock astonishment. "You're naked again. Just the way I like you."

She squealed in surprise when he wrapped his hands around her waist and bent slightly to lift her onto one shoulder.

"Chase! What are you doing?"

"Turning caveman," he responded without apology.

Stalking to the bed, he flipped her over and dropped her unceremoniously in the middle of the king-size mattress. She bounced on the tight springs and giggled as she couldn't remember doing since she was a little girl.

Taking two steps to the side, Chase grabbed the bottle of Cristal by its long neck and then hopped on top of her, pinning her in place.

"This time," he said, his tone leaving no question of his intent, "I want to see how champagne tastes when I sip it from your belly button."

"All right," she agreed, stretching out, ready to once again be a part of this man's dessert. "As long as I can do the same to you."

Six

The next morning Chase got up even earlier than usual, slipping out of the bedroom while Elena was still asleep. He closed the connecting doors so nothing he said would be overheard, then set about rescheduling his appointments for the day. It wasn't an easy task, considering most of the meetings had been set up weeks in advance and it was earlier than most of his associates' offices opened.

But by the time Elena made an appearance—once again wearing the short, sexy green nightie and matching robe that accentuated the emerald of her eyes—his day was clear and he was ready to put his plan into motion.

Although he was chomping at the bit to get going, he tried his best to act normal. He sipped his coffee and read the paper. When she pressed him to eat breakfast, he grumbled, but managed to down a couple of sausage patties and half of the western omelet she transferred from her plate to his.

An hour later, he rose from the table and repeated his speech from the day before, telling her he would be busy until dinnertime and that she should go out and have fun, at his expense. He handed her the same gold card and pile of cash she'd left on the dresser yesterday.

Out in the hall, he took the elevator to the lobby, but instead of leaving the hotel the way he normally would, he found a spot behind a bank of slot machines where he could keep an eye on the entrance without being seen.

He waited longer than he'd expected, checking his watch every few minutes. It took more than an hour for Elena to finally step off the elevator and head for the re- volving doors leading outside.

She wore brown chunky heels, loose linen slacks the color of sunflowers and a form-fitting top with renaissance sleeves. Dark-tinted sunglasses were perched atop her head, and she carried a good size tan tote on one shoulder.

Hopping up from his stool, Chase followed her, staying a fair distance behind so she wouldn't spot him. She stopped on the sidewalk, pulling the sunglasses down to shade her eyes from the bright mid-morning sun as she glanced in both directions, then started walking.

It seemed to Chase that they strolled down the street for an awfully long time. The sidewalks were already crowded, tourists flooding in and out of casinos and store- fronts. Perspiration beaded his brow and pooled inside his thousand-dollar designer suit.

He was no stranger to working up a sweat, having

grown up on a working ranch in Texas, where it could get just as hot as Nevada. Even though he'd chosen a different path and had more money than Croesus, he still enjoyed spending the day helping his parents or brother on their connecting properties. Currying horses, shucking hay, fixing fences… He just didn't usually do any of those things in a fine Italian suit that cost more than his brother's favorite saddle.

If Elena didn't get to where she was going soon, he was going to give up and flag down a taxi to take him back to the Wynn.

Almost as soon as he thought it, she turned into a storefront. He stayed outside, trying to catch a glimpse of her through the giant plate glass windows.

So she was shopping, after all, he thought. The confusing part was that it wasn't a fancy boutique, didn't carry shoes or jewelry or designer clothes. It was a candy and toy store, full of fun, colorful products that would have had any child squealing with joy.

Elena strolled up and down the aisles, studying the bins of candy and chocolate, the racks of water pistols, action figures and plastic princess jewelry. When a clerk came up to her, she smiled and started pointing at certain items, nodding when the woman seemed to understand what she was interested in.

What the heck was she doing? Chase wondered. He adjusted his own sunglasses and tried to get a better look without being tagged as a stalker.

He watched as she stacked toys on the checkout counter, the other woman filling bags with assorted candies at Elena's instruction. By the time they finished, her pile would have put Willy Wonka and his legendary Chocolate Factory to shame.

The clerk scanned everything, rang up the total and Elena handed over a credit card. But it wasn't a gold one, so it obviously wasn't his.

Rather than take plastic bags with the store's logo on them, she put everything into her own tan tote, thanked the woman behind the counter with a wave and headed back toward the street.

Chase whipped around and hurried to the storefront right next door. This time, she flagged down a cab, and he suffered a moment of panic worrying he might lose her. Then, when he caught a taxi of his own, he felt like the headliner of a bad action movie, ordering the driver, "Follow that car!" The hundred-dollar bill Chase flashed kept the driver from commenting or looking at him as though he had a few screws loose.

Several minutes later, they pulled up in front of a large gray brick building surrounded by a tall chain-link fence. Chase watched from half a block away as Elena got out of her cab and slipped through the closed gate. He asked his driver to wait, then hurried along to see just what she was up to.

He didn't have to go far. She hadn't actually gone into the building after passing through the gate, but was seated on the bench seat of a red plastic picnic table at the edge of what looked like a school's play yard.

Staying back, he watched kids of all ages crowding around her, and she was smiling and laughing, making a point of reaching out to touch each one on the head, the cheek, the arm.

Something lurched deep in his gut at the sight of her looking so happy. She was talking, teasing, her hands moving a mile a minute, then reaching into her bag for the things she'd bought at the store.

It took him a moment to realize the children weren't as noisy as he would have expected, and that Elena's animated hand motions weren't simply a side effect of her exuberant mood.

She was speaking in sign language. The children bustling around her couldn't hear. Chase looked around and his eyes lit on the sign on the front of the building that labeled it a school for the deaf. Yet Elena was inter-acting with them as easily as she would anyone else... perhaps better.

Oh, no, he didn't want to see this. Didn't even want to know about it.

He spun around, glancing at the taxi waiting for him at the curb, then turned back.

The kids loved her, loved the goodies she'd brought them, loved the attention.

And he hated it, because the entire situation was living, breathing proof that Elena wasn't the same shallow, vapid girl he'd known nearly twenty years ago.

His mind in turmoil, he whirled around again and stormed to the cab, ordering the driver to take him back to the hotel. He fumed the whole way, stopping just short of ranting to himself and removing any doubt from the cabbie's mind that he was a few quarters short of a roll.

He didn't want to deal with any of this, didn't want to see Elena as a sweet, thoughtful woman who knew sign language and would choose to spend her days in Las

Vegas entertaining a group of differently-abled children rather than shopping and running up his credit card bill.

Had he ever met another woman who would do the same? His mother and sister-in-law, maybe, but they didn't count.

What was he going to say to Elena when she got back tonight? He didn't think he could look at her the same as he had that morning. Or touch her without remembering the sight of her with those children.

Because Chase had been so upset the day before when she'd returned a little late from her outing, Elena made a point of getting back early this time. She was hot and sticky and looking forward to taking a quick shower before she needed to start getting ready for dinner.

To her surprise, the suite was empty when she got there. She'd expected to find Chase at the desk, clacking away at his laptop, or in the bedroom getting dressed. Instead, as she checked each room and even called for him, he was nowhere to be found. And he hadn't left a note to let her know where he was or when he'd be back…at least none she could find.

Well, maybe he was still working or one of his appointments had run long.

She dropped her tote in a corner, left her sunglasses on the narrow kitchenette countertop and headed for the bathroom.

Half an hour later, she emerged fresh and clean, with one towel wrapped around her wet hair and another tucked above her breasts. She was humming, off in her own little world, and didn't realize Chase was in the room until she glanced up and saw him standing on the other side of the wide, neatly made bed.

was the last thing she wanted. For a brief second, s
idered running for the bathroom and locking hers
ut that would be the coward's way out, and she did
t to be a coward. She just didn't want to deal with h
n any time in the near future.

he door opened, then closed, and she heard h
ing across the carpeted room in her direction. It to
f her willpower not to turn her head and scowl at hi
she kept her attention on the TV, pretending to
ply absorbed in the crime drama playing on the scre
The closer Chase got to the sofa, the more her sl
gled, every hair standing on end. And still she refus
acknowledge him.

"Elena," he said after a moment.

His voice was tight and clipped, but she refused
pond.

"Elena," he repeated, more softly this time. "Won't y
least look at me?"

She clenched her teeth to keep from saying someth
y scathing, and instead punched the remote contro
up the volume a couple more notches.

"Dammit, Elena." Chase leaned down, entering
on for the first time, and snatched the remote from
. He tossed it onto the seat of a nearby chair, well
r reach.

arely managing to hold on to her temper, she slid
d legs off the couch and stood, moving away fr
o skirt the low coffee table. She made it just a
from the bedroom door before he stopped her
ing her arm.

e opened her mouth to give him a piece of her m

She jumped, pressing a hand to her heart. "Good Lord, you scared me," she said with a light laugh.

A little thrill went through her at the sight of him. He looked more handsome than any man had a right to be in his navy suit, his dark hair smoothly styled, a splash of color spilling down his chest from his tie. She was even getting used to his intense blue eyes and unsmiling mouth.

"You should have knocked on the bathroom door or given a yell when you got back so I'd know you were here." Moving to the dresser, she started opening and closing drawers, pulling out an assortment of under-clothes. "I won't be long. I was just about to get ready."

"Don't bother."

His words, as well as the coldness in his tone, gave her pause. She stopped what she was doing, a pair of dia-phanous black, French-cut panties dangling from her fingertips.

"Excuse me?" she said, telling herself not to let her imagination run away with her.

Chase Ramsey wasn't exactly the warmest person she'd ever met—he might have had a bad meeting and was taking his lousy mood out on her.

"We have another dinner tonight, right? Don't you want me to dress to the nines and impress all your business associates?" She grinned and twitched her hips seductively.

His expression didn't change. He still looked like he was contemplating something particularly unsavory.

"*I* have a dinner meeting," he finally replied, his voice like a splash of ice water on her already wet and chilled body. "Your presence isn't required."

He rounded the bed, leaving enough space for a tractor trailer to park between them as he passed. "I'll be back in a few hours."

She stood where she was, stunned by his announcement and abrupt departure. From the other room, she heard the door of the suite open and then slam shut, and knew she was alone.

Why in heaven's name would Chase suddenly decide that he didn't need her with him, when that was his sole reason for blackmailing her and bringing her along?

And what was with his attitude? He could be a hard man, distant and cruel at times. At least with her; she didn't know how he acted with his family or friends. But she also knew why he treated her that way, and that—in his mind—she deserved it.

But lately, since they'd been here in Las Vegas, sharing this enormous, lavish suite, he'd been different. She'd thought that he was beginning to soften toward her, that they were beginning to connect.

And, she admitted, she'd begun to develop feelings for him.

She wouldn't go so far as to say she was in love with him, since she wasn't sure it was possible to be in love with a man whose mind was set on revenge against her. But she had started to be kind of glad he'd manipulated her into becoming his lover. She doubted they ever would have gotten together otherwise, and now that she'd spent so much time alone with him, she realized she wouldn't be opposed to a relationship with him.

Chase apparently had other ideas. From the way he'd treated her just now, it seemed he not only didn't want her

to accompany him to dinner, but mig around anymore at all.

Swallowing hard, she let the barely-th back in the drawer and slammed it clo marched into the bathroom, dropped the to hair and chest and shrugged into one of the b cloth robes the hotel provided.

She'd never worn one of them before, opti the sexier sleep sets she'd brought along. Eve packed was sexy, because that was what sl Chase would want.

Well, to hell with him. From now on, she w comfort, wear what she wanted, without a tho likes or dislikes.

It's not as though he would be touching her anyway. If he so much as tried, she'd break his kick him where it hurt.

Stalking into the sitting room, she grabbe service menu, found about twelve things that petizing, and ordered them all. Ha! She mig used the credit card he gave her, but she sur up his room charges.

She spent the rest of the evening curled u stuffed sofa, stuffing her face and flip channels on the television. Nothing seeme interest, and no amount of food seemed burning in her gut.

It was close to nine o'clock when she he of the key card on the other side of the do lurched and every muscle in her bod prepared herself to face Chase.

only to have him spin her around, pin her to the nearest wall with his imposing bulk and mash his lips to hers.

With a moan of outrage, she pushed at his shoulders, turned from side to side trying to wiggle away. He merely tightened his hold until his hard chest pressed against the growing tautness of her nipples, his strong thighs trapping hers.

And then the pressure of his mouth changed. Lightening, growing more cajoling than demanding. She moaned again, this time in surrender.

Her nails dug into his shoulders, pulling him closer rather than attempting to push him away, and her leg snaked up to wrap around one of his. His hands spanned her waist as he tore his mouth away, his lips moving to her chin, her throat, the curve of her ear.

"I'm sorry," he panted, the words vibrating over her skin and into her bones. "I acted like an ass earlier. I was in a bad mood and took it out on you. I shouldn't have, and I'm sorry."

Her brain was turning to liquid, as was the rest of her body. She could barely remember what he'd said to her all those hours ago, let alone how upset she'd been with him afterward.

"Forgive me?"

His fingers fumbled with the thick belt of her robe, getting it open and pushing apart the edges of the heavy terry cloth. She was naked beneath and the cool air of the suite washed over her rapidly heating flesh. He fastened his mouth on the straining tip of one breast and she whimpered, digging her fingers into his hair to hold him in place.

How could she deny him when he made her blood flow like molten lava and drove every rational thought from her head?

"Yes," she said breathlessly. "Yes, yes."

He moved to her other breast and she gasped, letting her head fall back against the wall as sensation after sensation washed over her. Reaching between them, he quickly undid his pants and lifted her legs around his waist, filling her in one long, strong stroke.

Biting her bottom lip to keep from crying out, Elena crossed her ankles behind his back, arched her back in an attempt to get even closer to him and let the ripples of pleasure wash over her.

He was so powerful. So confident and masculine and…incredible. No one had ever had such a profound effect on her before. And she doubted anyone ever would again.

Chase's breathing sounded in her ear, heavy and harsh to match her own. It took only moments for the intensity to build, for the desire spiraling in her belly to grow almost unbearable and for her to shatter into a million little pieces, taking Chase over the precipice with her into ecstasy.

They clung to each other, gasping for air, then slowly slid down the wall to the floor in a tangle of limbs and disheveled clothes.

Several minutes later, his chest rumbled with a low chuckle. He shifted slightly, moving into a more comfortable position and bringing her with him to rest in the crook of his arm. "Guess I understand now why make-up sex has such a stellar reputation. Maybe later, we can get into another fight and do that again."

She gave an exhausted, wheezing laugh, positive she would never have enough energy to argue *or* make love with quite that much exuberance again. She'd be surprised if she could even manage to walk on her own two legs before early next week.

Seven

Standing in the corner of the huge, crowded ballroom, Chase buried his hands in his pants pockets and scuffed his booted foot on the highly polished floor. Adults were milling all over, drinking, laughing, nibbling on little finger sandwiches and chunks of cheese speared with fancy toothpicks.

At least that's what he thought they were eating. When they'd first come in, he'd taken a good look at some of the trays the waiters were carrying around and decided there was nothing on them he'd be putting in his mouth.

The big, expensive house was decorated for Christmas within an inch of its life. Santas, reindeer, holly boughs, snowflakes, bells, angels, mistletoe…if it had anything to do with Christmas, it was stuffed somewhere in this mausoleum.

He hated this sort of thing. If his mom and dad hadn't made him come to this stupid party, at this stupid old mansion, he would be home right now, watching TV or doing chores in the barn with his brother.

But from some of the whispered conversations he'd overheard between his parents, things hadn't been great with their family lately, financially speaking. Victor Sanchez had hired his dad to do some work with his horses and paid him well for his expertise, so when the man invited the Ramseys to his home for a huge holiday celebration, it would have been rude—according to Chase's mother—not to accept.

But he still didn't see why he and Mitch had had to come along. If his parents wanted to schmooze and make a good impression, fine, but this was nothing but a waste of time for him.

There were hardly any other teenagers in attendance and those who were looked to be stuck-up snobs. He recognized a few of them from school, all part of the "in" crowd—while he and his brother definitely weren't.

Not that he was complaining. He liked his life, liked living on a horse and cattle ranch and helping his father out every chance he got. If he had his way, he'd drop out of school altogether and spend his days working with the animals and riding his favorite gelding, Skywalker.

And he'd never have to dress up in a ridiculous suit, with a tie just about strangling him to death. He tugged at his shirt collar, trying again to loosen the darn thing before it cut off his air supply.

There was only one person here he was even kind of interested in being around, and that was Mr. Sanchez's daughter, Elena. She was a year or two younger than Chase, and he saw her around school once in a while, but they definitely didn't run in the same crowd.

The Sanchezes were rich.

The Ramseys weren't.

Elena Sanchez was gorgeous and popular.

Chase didn't exactly look like he'd been hit in the face with a brick, but girls like her didn't hang around boys who wore faded jeans, dusty boots and beat-up cowboy hats.

Of course, that didn't mean boys in faded jeans and Stetsons didn't enjoy watching pretty girls in their pricey clothes.

And Chase had watched Elena plenty. Not that he'd admit to such a fact, even if his brother put him in a headlock and threatened to dunk him in the disgusting, algae-covered water trough he hadn't gotten around to cleaning yet.

Chase huffed a nervous, indecisive breath and tapped the heel of his boot a couple more times on the floor. He'd never have the courage to go up to her at school, with so many other kids around, but maybe here he could.

This was a Christmas party. Everyone was in a festive and possibly more receptive mood than usual.

So maybe...

Glancing around, he took a couple tentative steps away from his post against the wall. His mother and father were chatting with another couple on the far side of the room. His brother was dancing with some older, attractive girl, smiling and swinging her around in the center of the area designated for just that purpose. An eight-piece orchestra was playing high-brow music, interspersed with the occasional holiday instrumental.

And over by the punch bowl stood Elena with a few of her friends. They looked familiar, too. He thought their first names were Tisha, Leslie, Stephanie and Candy, but wasn't sure of their last names. Not that the specifics mattered; they were all part of the country club set.

He took the long way around, skirting the crowd, scuffling his feet when he should have been taking long, confident strides. But his brother was the smooth one with girls. Chase liked them well enough, and most of the time, they liked him back, but they also tended to be the tomboy type and were more friends than girlfriends.

Elena definitely wasn't the tomboy type, but she would be the first girl he'd asked to dance…if he ever got around to it.

He was at the edge of the buffet table now, only a yard or two away from her. A man walked past, bumping into Chase without apologizing or even acknowledging the slight. Typical of this crowd, Chase thought. If you weren't one of their own—namely rich and powerful—then you might as well not exist.

Shaking off the thought, he took a deep breath, pulled his hands from his pockets and stepped forward.

It took a moment for Elena to notice him. She was dressed in a pretty red velvet dress with white lace trim. One side of her long black hair was pulled up and pinned in place with a sprig of live holly.

Her friends, however, noticed him right away. The four of them fixed him with cold, snooty stares, as though he'd just tromped in from the cow barn, covered head to toe in manure.

He ignored them, keeping his attention firmly locked on Elena.

"Hey," he said, sliding his hands back into the front pockets of his dress pants, bunching up the bottom of his matching jacket.

She glanced at him, then at her friends, then back to him. "Hello."

Her response could have been warmer, but it wasn't exactly glacial, either. He pressed on.

"Um... are you having fun?"

Another shifted look to her friends. Her expression remained impassive, not terribly interested, but also not as offended as the others in her little clique.

"Yes."

Dragging his hands from his pockets, he straightened his suit coat and wiped his palms on the sides of his slacks.

"So, do you want to dance?" he asked on a rush, feeling his face heat and resisting the urge to yank at his tie.

Her brows rose and she slanted a sideways glance at her girlfriends, who now had their arms crossed over their chests and were scowling at him. One of them threw her head back and laughed.

Chase almost told her she sounded like one of his father's mares when she whinnied, but at the moment he was more concerned with Elena's answer to his question.

Elena gave a snort, crossing her arms and hitching a hip in a perfect replication of her friends' poses. "I don't think so," she told him in a snotty, highfalutin tone.

Her green eyes flitted down to the floor, taking in the pair of cowboy boots he was wearing. They were his best pair, black and polished to a shine, but they were still boots instead of leather dress shoes.

She lifted her head, once again meeting his gaze. "Why don't you go dance with one of your horses?"

Her friends burst into hoots of laughter, huddling

together to share their amusement at his audacity in daring to approach one of their own.

Chase felt as though he'd been doused with a bucket of ice water. His cheeks heated and his stomach lurched sickeningly.

Without another word, he turned and shouldered his way through the crowd, rushing outside into the chilly night air. Even in Texas, the nights could get cold, especially in December.

But he didn't care; he wasn't going back inside. He would sit in the car and wait for his parents and brother to decide to leave the party, but no matter how cold or hungry he might get, he wasn't going back in that big house—or anywhere near Elena Sanchez ever again.

Hours after their frantic, explosive coupling against the sitting room wall, Chase and Elena were wrapped around each other in the center of the king-size bed, sheets tangled about their naked bodies. The muted noises of the outside world mingled with their breathing to lull them both to sleep.

Chase honestly hadn't thought his legs would ever work again, never mind other parts of his anatomy. He'd thought he'd expire right there on the carpeted floor—sweaty, drained, clothes askew, with Elena sprawled half on top and half beneath him.

But within the hour, he'd somehow found the strength to climb to his feet and help Elena to hers, too.

He hadn't intended to do anything more than get her into bed, but then he'd caught a glimpse of her flushed skin and her half-exposed breasts through the opening of her fluffy white robe, and he'd realized that where Elena

Sanchez was concerned, there was no such thing as being completely exhausted—or completely sated.

He'd started kissing her in the doorway of the bedroom, and before they'd crossed the threshold, they were tearing their clothes off the rest of the way and stumbling for the bed.

Now they were once again pleasantly worn out, and— for the moment, anyway—satisfied. She was tucked along his side, her head on his shoulder, one leg thrown across his thigh. Her breathing was shallow and even, and her long, midnight hair fell over his arm like an expensive silk scarf.

She was probably sleeping. After everything he'd put her through this evening, he wouldn't blame her if she slept straight through the rest of their time in Vegas.

And he sort of hoped she was, because after what he'd seen earlier that day, and all the old memories that had been assaulting him ever since, he couldn't seem to stop himself from saying, "I saw you this afternoon."

He felt her inhale sharply in startlement, then shift closer, her chin rubbing absently against the top of his chest.

"Hmm?"

He held his breath, waiting to see if she would wake up or slip back into unconsciousness, and didn't know which he wished for more.

She continued to wiggle around, making it hard for him to remember that they'd already made love twice that night. And then she lifted her head, blinking like an owl as she struggled toward wakefulness.

"I'm sorry," she said, covering a yawn with her hand. "What did you say?"

In for a penny, in for a pound, he thought.

If offer card is missing write to: Silhouette Reader Service, 3010 Walden Ave., P.O. Box 1867, Buffalo NY 14240-1867

NO POSTAGE
NECESSARY
IF MAILED
IN THE
UNITED STATES

BUSINESS REPLY MAIL
FIRST-CLASS MAIL   PERMIT NO. 717-003   BUFFALO, NY

POSTAGE WILL BE PAID BY ADDRESSEE

SILHOUETTE READER SERVICE
3010 WALDEN AVE
PO BOX 1867
BUFFALO NY 14240-9952

Do You Have the LUCKY KEY?

PLAY THE *Lucky Key Game*

and you can get

FREE BOOKS and FREE GIFTS!

Scratch the gold areas with a coin. Then check below to see the books and gifts you can get!

YES!

I have scratched off the gold areas. Please send me the **2 FREE BOOKS** and **2 FREE GIFTS** for which I qualify. I understand I am under no obligation to purchase any books, as explained on the back of this card.

(S-D-02/07)

326 SDL EF5Q   **225 SDL EF6G**

FIRST NAME	LAST NAME

ADDRESS

APT.#   CITY

STATE/ PROV.   ZIP/POSTAL CODE

www.eHarlequin.com

🔑🔑🔑🔑 2 free books plus 2 free gifts   🔑🔑🔑🔑 1 free book

🔑🔑🔑🔑 2 free books   🔑🔑🔑🔑 Try Again!

Offer limited to one per household and not valid to current Silhouette Desire® subscribers.
Your Privacy – Silhouette is committed to protecting your privacy. Our Privacy Policy is available online at www.eHarlequin.com or upon request from the Silhouette Reader Service. From time to time we make our lists of customers available to reputable firms who may have a product or service of interest to you. If you would prefer for us not to share your name and address, please check here. ☐

"I saw you this afternoon," he repeated, careful to keep his tone flat, indifferent. "In the school yard."

A beat passed while he watched emotions play over her face. Shock, guilt, uncertainty. It only lasted a second, though, before her features settled back to their usual calm.

"I thought you were in meetings all day," she said by way of response. Pulling the covers up to her neck, she settled more comfortably, still snug at his side.

"I was supposed to be. But I wanted to see where you went."

"Why?"

She didn't sound angry or annoyed, simply curious. Which allowed him to admit the truth without feeling self-conscious.

"You didn't use my money or charge anything to my credit card yesterday." He shrugged. "I wanted to know what you were doing with your time in Sin City without spending a dime."

"I spent a dime," she corrected. "Quite a few of them. It just happened to be my money instead of yours."

She slid around, straightening her leg to rest between both of his and splaying herself more fully across his chest. Propping her chin on top of her hands, she met his gaze and said, "Although, I did use some of your cash for a cab and a bit of lunch yesterday. Hope you don't mind."

A flicker of annoyance flashed through his system. She was being purposely obtuse.

"I don't care about the money. I wouldn't have given it to you if I did. I want to know what you were doing at a school for deaf children, when most women with an unlimited line of someone else's credit would have cleared out every boutique in a ten-mile radius."

One corner of her mouth twisted up in a mocking grin. "What kind of girl do you take me for?"

"A spoiled, self-absorbed debutante," he replied, not even needing to think about it. Pain flickered across her eyes, but he wouldn't let himself be moved by the reaction.

With a sigh, she pushed away from him and sat up, taking the satin sheet with her.

"You're right. That's exactly what I was. Maybe I still am, I don't know."

He watched her cross her legs and fold the sheet more fully around her body, moving just far enough on the wide, firm mattress that they were no longer touching. Using his forearms, he pushed himself into a sitting position, stuffing an extra pillow behind his back so he could recline against the headboard.

"You're a social worker. You know sign language. And you somehow managed to find probably the only special-needs school within the city limits on your first day in town. None of those are things I ever would have expected from the girl I knew in junior high."

"Well, to be honest, I've known about the school for years. A friend of mine used to teach there, and even though she doesn't live in Nevada anymore, I still like to drop by and spend time with the kids whenever I'm in the area."

She clutched the sheet tighter against her breasts and readjusted her legs. The fire engine-red polish on her toenails peeked out briefly before disappearing again.

"And a lot has happened since we were teenagers. A lot has changed."

Enough to turn a cruel, selfish brat into a kind, selfless woman? He wasn't sure he believed such a drastic shift in personality was possible.

"I know this is almost twenty years too late," she said softly, "but I'm sorry for the way I treated you at that Christmas party when we were kids. You're right—I was spoiled and selfish and every other nasty word you can think of. My parents had money and were important in the community, and I thought that made me rich and important, too." Her usually bright eyes darkened, and for a moment, she wouldn't meet his gaze. "But it only made me a bitch."

Since that was exactly what he'd always thought of her, he didn't bother trying to correct her or make her feel better. It was only slightly gratifying to hear her admit the same.

"What I said to you that night…it was cruel and unnecessary and unforgivable. And even though I know it can't make up for the pain and humiliation I caused you, I am sorry."

Chase gritted his teeth, his hands fisting unconsciously at his sides. Moisture played along her lashes, adding sincerity to her already heartfelt words. But he'd be damned if he'd let a few tears and a long overdue apology convince him that she'd turned over a new leaf and no longer possessed any of those negative, stuck-up teenage traits.

"So what happened to bring about this remarkable transformation?" he asked, his voice sounding acerbic even to his own ears.

Her answer, when it came, was short and without embellishment—and immediately made him feel like a first-class heel.

"My mother died."

Lips thinning, he muttered a curse. "I'm sorry."

"Thank you," she murmured quietly. The long curtain of her hair hid her face as she turned her gaze to her lap, toying with a corner of the sheet.

"She was sick for quite a while, and that sort of experience changes a person. One minute, I was a carefree prima donna, and the next my whole world was falling apart. That's when I realized the whole world didn't revolve around my wants and needs, and that there are more important things in life than money or social status."

He wasn't sure he agreed with that sentiment. He'd spent his entire adult life working to make money and build his social status in an attempt to prove to the Elenas of the world that he wasn't just a poor rancher's son. He was an industrious businessman, who—in recent years, at least—had become one of the wealthiest men in Texas.

It was no small coincidence that the Ramsey Corporation happened to be the company poised to overtake Sanchez Restaurant Supply. Chase had been keeping an eye on Elena's family for years, not only so he would know when he'd surpassed them financially, but in hopes that just such an opportunity would present itself.

He wanted nothing more than to thumb his nose at them—at Elena—and show them all what he'd become. Not just a stinking rich tycoon in his own right, but a man to be respected and admired.

Which didn't explain why he was suddenly feeling pangs of guilt over his plans for revenge against this woman.

So she'd suffered a loss. Didn't everyone at some point in their lives?

So he found her irresistible in bed. What red-blooded American male wouldn't?

It didn't make her a saint, and it didn't make him a bad guy.

"The things I'd always thought were so important," she continued, "weren't anymore. And no amount of my father's wealth or prestige could make my mother better. She had the best medical care money could buy and still it wasn't enough."

"So you became a social worker," he said, tamping down on the sympathies threatening to overwhelm his better senses. "To try to save the world in other ways?"

"Not save the world," she said softly. "But I did want to help people. Our family has more than enough money to get by. Even if we lost the business—which I don't want us to do because of how important it is to my father—" she added with a meaningful glance, "we'd still be okay financially. I wanted to do something with my life that made a difference."

"And I'll bet you do. Make a difference, I mean."

A small smile played over her face. "I try. There are so many kids in trouble out there, so many families with problems. I just do what I can—and what the law allows— to make things a little better for them."

"And you don't turn down awkward teenage boys when they ask you to dance, just because their parents aren't as rich as yours?"

She flushed, her cheeks turning pink with embarrassment. "I'm not sure how many teenage boys would ask me to dance these days, but no. I wouldn't turn anyone down based on their upbringing or bank account. Especially you."

"But I've got money now," he pointed out, arching a brow. "Doesn't that make me more acceptable?"

"No more and no less. I don't judge people that way anymore and I never should have to begin with."

Wiggling around the bed, she pulled the sheet with her as she once again took up position along his side, one leg draped over his thigh, her breasts pressing into his chest.

"At the risk of making you even angrier about that night," she told him, turning her head to rest on his shoulder, "I really did think you were cute back then. If it hadn't been for my friends and my fear of what they might say, I probably would have danced with you—and enjoyed every minute of it."

He didn't reply; instead he let the room fall into silence and her words sink deep into his bones. Beside him, Elena's breathing turned deep and even, and he knew she'd fallen asleep.

But Chase couldn't sleep; his mind wouldn't let him. Into the wee hours of the night, he stayed awake, trying to make sense of what she'd told him, of the thoughts and feelings ricocheting through him like a pinball in an arcade game. No matter how hard he tried, he couldn't seem to reconcile this "new" Elena with the memories he had of her and the woman he'd expected her to be.

All he knew was that the emotions *this* Elena was churning up inside him made him distinctly uncomfortable.

Eight

The next few days in Las Vegas passed easily. Chase spent his days in business meetings, while Elena made one more trip to play with the children at the hearing-impaired school, then did a bit of window shopping. She sent postcards to some friends, even knowing she'd likely be home before they arrived. And she bought a pair of silver and amethyst swing earrings for Alandra from a boutique in the Wynn.

In the evenings she would accompany Chase to any dinner functions he needed to attend. Once or twice, they even ordered in, eating from the room service cart while they sat in front of the television in nightgown and boxer shorts.

And at night, they made love.

There was no more talk of that Christmas dance at her parents' house nearly twenty years ago, or the type of person she'd been as a teen. Chase seemed satisfied with the answers she'd given him about her mother's death and her change of heart. At least for the moment.

Elena didn't try to fool herself into believing that the past was entirely dead and buried, of course. She was afraid the hurt she'd caused him by turning him down so rudely in front of her friends ran too deeply to be forgiven overnight. But she was happy to go on the way things were running now. Spending time with him, sharing less volatile memories of their school days and mutual acquaintances, sleeping each night in his arms.

It was the last one that caused her the most turmoil. Because she was just a bit *too* comfortable with him. Enjoyed making love with him a bit *too* much. Found herself forgetting the exact details of their arrangement a bit *too* often.

It was just so easy to pretend they were a normal couple, spending a week together out of town and getting to know each other better. No deals or arrangements involved. No blackmail to get her there, no guilt driving her to do whatever she could to save her father's business.

A big part of her *wanted* to be there. And worse, she wished it were real.

How could this have happened? How could she have gone from resenting him for blackmailing her to share his bed, to wondering how she was going to feel when their arrangement was over?

It wouldn't be easy. Already, her chest felt tight and her eyes stung whenever she thought about the time when they would go their separate ways.

That moment was closing in fast.

She finished folding a knit dress and tucked it into her suitcase, trying not to think about what would happen next.

Chase was at his last meeting of the week in Las Vegas. He'd packed his things earlier, then left her behind in the room to do the same. Their flight back to Texas was scheduled for after lunch.

And that, she thought, was when it would all be over.

She took a deep breath, patting her clothes down before heading to the bathroom for her toiletries.

If, in the week she'd been gone, her father had managed to get enough money together to save SRS, then there would be no reason for her relationship with Chase to continue. He would have nothing to hold over her head and no leverage to demand she remain his mistress.

How pathetic was it that the prospect saddened her? That she actually *wanted* her father to be having trouble getting his finances and backers together so she could have an excuse to remain with Chase just a bit longer.

Her sister would have a fit if she knew what Elena was thinking. Alandra would put her hands on her hips and shake her head, then launch into a lengthy lecture about Elena standing up for herself and not letting a man dictate her moods. If she wanted to be with Chase Ramsey, then she should simply tell him that she didn't want their relationship to end once her father managed to save SRS. She should tell him she wanted to be more than just his mistress. How much more, she wasn't sure, but she would at least like the time and opportunity to see where things led.

But, oh, wouldn't Chase love that. His feelings for her were already bitter enough; all he needed to send them right into pure hatred was to have her announce that she might be falling in love with him and didn't want to let him go after their deal was done.

She released a brittle chuckle as she dumped bottles of lotions and shampoos into her suitcase, closed the lid and zipped it shut.

Oh, yes, he'd just love that. The woman he'd blackmailed into being his mistress suddenly got too attached and wanted more. Wouldn't that just shoot his plan for revenge all to hell.

From the other room, she heard the door to the suite click open and then close. She took a deep breath and blinked a few times, fighting to get her emotions under control before he came in and noticed how close she was to falling apart.

"Hey," he said, tossing the key card on the dresser.

Smiling a bit too widely, Elena turned to greet him. "Hey."

"You all packed?"

"I just finished," she said, patting one of her bags.

"Good. If you want, we can have the bags taken down, then get some lunch before we head for the airport."

She nodded. "Fine with me."

She started to pull her bags and suitcase off the bed, moving them closer to the doorway, where he was leaning against the jamb.

"One other thing before we go," he murmured, taking the handle of the wheeled case, the larger of the two bags, from her. Turning, he headed for the main door and propped her luggage with his own.

"Yes?" she asked distractedly, hitching the strap of her purse on her shoulder as she followed along behind and set her smaller carry-on bag next to the rest. She straightened to find him watching her intently, his blue eyes shining like crystals behind dark lashes.

He took her arm, his fingers banding firmly just above her elbow. "When we get back," he told her slowly, "if your father hasn't come up with the resources necessary to pull SRS out of the fire, I'll expect you to continue with our agreement. Unless, of course, you're no longer concerned with helping Victor save the family business."

The latter seemed to be half apology, half threat. Elena thought she should probably be offended, or at least act outraged that he would dictate her actions once they returned home to Gabriel's Crossing.

Instead, she felt almost elated. Ten days wasn't very long to collect the kind of money her father needed to stave off the Ramsey Corporation, which meant the chances were pretty good that they *would* need to buy more time. Time she'd be required to remain with Chase.

That had been the deal, after all. She would play the part of his mistress for as long as it took for her father to raise the funds to save SRS. Just because they would no longer be a practically anonymous couple in the bright lights of Las Vegas didn't mean she could go back on her word.

Taking a deep breath, she met his gaze and nodded. "Of course. I only ask that we be discreet. My family and the rest of world don't need to know the details of why we'll suddenly be spending so much time together."

He inclined his head, his fingers dropping from her arm. "Agreed."

With that, he turned to open the door and she felt a wave of relief wash through her. She would be spending more time with Chase, after all, rather than being tossed aside like an old pair of gym socks as soon as their plane landed in Texas.

And if she also felt more than a small jab of guilt at hoping it took her father awhile longer to move the family back into the black, she would deal with that later.

They'd been home nearly a week when Chase called Elena at work. She hadn't spoken to him since he'd dropped her off at the house she shared with her father and sister the afternoon they'd returned from Las Vegas.

She'd wondered about him, caught herself jumping whenever the phone rang, half hoping he was calling to demand she spend the night with him. Or even that she accompany him to some dinner or another.

But he hadn't, and since she hadn't given him her work number, she'd never expected him to call her there. Of course, she should have known that a man like Chase Ramsey could find her wherever she was, if he put his mind to it.

As always, he got right to the point.

"My mother invited me to dinner tonight. My brother is going to be there with his wife and daughter and I thought you might like to go and meet everyone." Before she could respond, he went on. "No problem if you already have other plans. I'll just tell Mom I'm in the middle of an important business deal and will be working all evening."

For a minute, Elena didn't know what to say. She clutched the phone to her ear, her mouth hanging open in surprise.

He wanted her to meet his family? And if she said no, he wasn't going to go at all?

What did that mean? Was he simply being polite, or did he have a more personal, hidden agenda?

Her mind was spinning, her heart racing a mile a minute.

"U-um," she stuttered before quickly shaking herself. "Yes, of course. I'd love to go."

"You're sure?" he asked, sounding almost sorry he'd called. "Because—"

"I'm sure. My evening is wide open."

It hadn't been, but it would be now. Her sister would understand. They had only been going to the mall, anyway. Something about looking for toys for the children at one of Alandra's charities.

"What time will you be picking me up? Or would you rather I met you there?"

"No, I'll pick you up. Let's say…six o'clock?"

"Six it is. I'll see you then."

"Good. Great. See you then."

The line went dead, leaving Elena to listen to the hum of the dial tone. Slowly, she lowered her arm to hang up, leaving her fingers curled around the earpiece. A second later, she put the phone back to her ear and jabbed out a number she knew by heart.

"Hello?" her sister answered after only two rings.

Elena spoke only one word: "Help."

What should a girl wear to dinner to meet her lover's parents and brother? Especially when they were only lovers because he'd blackmailed her into bed.

That might not be the full reason she was staying in his bed, but it was certainly how he'd gotten her there to begin with.

Thankfully, she had a sister who was much more savvy about this sort of thing and knew the answers to these kinds of questions. As soon as Elena had called Alandra's cell phone with her semi-desperate plea, her sister had dropped everything and met her at home for a full sweep of both their closets.

It was only dinner at his parents' house, so nothing fancy was required. Instead, she needed something casual but elegant. Attractive and becoming without looking as though she'd worked at it.

Formal would have been easier, she soon realized. If she were attending a black-tie affair, she would simply have had to throw on something long and sequined with a pair of high heels. But dressing for dinner with Chase's family bordered on cruel and unusual punishment.

They immediately crossed blue jeans off the list for being too casual. And a dress of any type for being too fancy. Skirts were borderline, depending on the style and design.

Finally, after two or three hours of feeling like the mannequin for a window designer with multiple personality disorder, Elena held her arms up while Alandra pulled yet another top over her head, then stood back to study her latest creation.

"I think we've got it," her sister announced, grinning as she pointed at the mirror for Elena to see for herself.

Elena sighed in relief as she saw that she looked almost perfect. Maybe a little overdressed, but not by much. Especially if Chase came straight from the office and was still wearing his usual suit and tie.

Alandra had decided on a pair of wide-legged black slacks, with one-inch plain black pumps and a periwinkle blue sweater set trimmed with red, white, and black embroidered flowers.

"Are you sure?" she asked, tugging at the hem of the sweater and turning left and right to view the full effect.

"Absolutely. You look gorgeous, but not like you're trying to impress anyone. If I were meeting my new boyfriend's parents for the first time, I'd wear that exact outfit."

Elena's heart shuddered at her sister's words. "He's not my boyfriend," she said softly, her mouth gone dry as she turned away from the mirror. She couldn't quite bring herself to meet Alandra's gaze, so she moved to the bed, busying herself with putting earlier discarded garments back on their hangers.

"You're right," her sister readily agreed. "He's way too cute to be just a 'boyfriend.' He's your red-hot secret lover."

Face flaming, she whirled in Alandra's direction, waving a hand and glancing frantically toward the open bedroom door.

"Shhh," she hissed, marching past her sister to shut the door to hopefully provide them with a bit more privacy. Just in case. "No one is supposed to know, remember? And it won't be a secret much longer if you keep talking about it at full volume."

She turned back in time to see Alandra roll her eyes toward the ceiling. "You're going to have to tell people eventually if you keep spending so much time with the man."

"I haven't spent any time with him. This is the first time he's called me all week."

"Yes, but you flew to Vegas with him and stayed there almost a week."

Elena crossed her arms beneath her breasts and tapped her foot on the carpeted floor in agitation. "I flew to Vegas on *business,*" she corrected. "No one knows I went with Chase or what we did while we were there."

"*I* know," Alandra murmured pointedly, crossing her arms in a mirror image of her sister's pose.

Elena raised a brow. "What are you saying? That you're going to blackmail me, too?"

Honestly, was she giving off pheromones to signal that she was ripe for the picking? She'd gone thirty-three years without being bribed or strong-armed into anything, and now she was about to be manipulated twice in the same month. And once by her sister, no less!

But Alandra quickly put the quash on any concerns about that.

"Of course not! What kind of sister do you think I am?"

Dropping her arms, she stalked forward and took Elena's hand, tugging her to the set of pastel-striped armchairs by the window.

When they were both seated, Alandra said, "I'm worried about you, Elena. First you tell me you're being coerced into sleeping with this guy to help Pop save the company. And I understood your reasons for going through with it, really I did. I'd have probably done the same thing. But now you're standing here nervous about meeting the man's parents and worrying over what to wear when you do. Do you realize what that means?"

Elena blinked. It meant she was nervous about meeting Chase's parents, and that she wasn't the ever self-assured fashion plate her sister was, didn't it?

"It means you care," Alandra informed her gently. "If this were just a business arrangement, you wouldn't care how you looked tonight. You'd have probably gone in the same outfit you wore to work today and not given it a second thought."

"That's not true. I care how I look," Elena protested, but the words came out with so little confidence, even she didn't believe it.

"Of course you do. But you looked fine in what you were wearing this morning. And that song you were humming when you got home from Vegas tells me you weren't exactly chained up in Chase Ramsey's bed all week, forced to be his love slave against your will. I think," Alandra added, tipping her head to the side, "things between you are starting to get serious."

Elena swallowed past the lump in her throat, her heart pounding like a kettledrum. Once again, she was reminded that she could keep no secrets from a sister who knew her so well. For better or worse, Alandra could see straight through any attempts at subterfuge.

The air shuddered from her lungs. Her shoulders slumped and she let her chin fall to her chest. "I'm in trouble," she admitted, barely loud enough to be heard.

Her sister leaned forward, her expression going serious as she laid a hand on Elena's knee. "You're in love with him?" she asked.

Elena shook her head, slowly, almost as though she couldn't quite believe it herself. "I don't know, but I think I'm close."

She raised her head and met her sister's understanding eyes as her own started to sting and grow damp. "I'm really, really close."

Nine

Between her nerves over meeting Chase's parents and her disturbing conversation with Alandra before leaving, Elena's stomach was in knots. Her palms were sweating, her knees were shaking and every once in a while, her chest tightened so much, she could barely draw a breath.

When Chase pulled up to the house at six on the dot, Elena made her sister stay in her room. The last thing she needed was for Alandra to race down the stairs to catch a glimpse of him or be caught peering around the corner like a child on Christmas morning, trying to catch Santa Claus piling presents under the tree.

But even though Alandra bided by her wishes and stayed out of sight, Elena knew she was watching from the upstairs window as Chase helped her into the car and they pulled away.

On the drive, she tried to make small talk, tried to respond with some modicum of sensibility when Chase spoke. But inside, her blood and muscles and bones felt as though they'd been touched by a live wire. She was surprised he didn't notice a glow in her eyes or sparks shooting from her fingertips.

The Ramsey ranch was on the other side of Gabriel's Crossing, but they still arrived much too soon for Elena's peace of mind. Chase's shiny silver luxury car bumped down a long, rutted dirt driveway, kicking up a cloud of dust behind them.

A dark blue pickup truck was already parked in front of the house. Chase pulled up beside it and cut the engine.

For a moment, they sat there, neither one making a move to get out. Elena stared at the front door, fully expecting it to fly open and the stuff of nightmares to pour out.

Alandra was right; it meant something. Despite her better judgment, she was falling for Chase, and falling hard. And for some reason, whether or not his parents liked her felt like a very big deal.

She wished it didn't. She wished she could convince herself that this was merely another business dinner he'd asked her to attend. Meeting his parents felt entirely too much like something a girlfriend would do.

A girlfriend, not a mistress.

The click of the door latch releasing on Chase's side of the car interrupted her thoughts and she hurried to open her own and climb to her feet. Brushing her hands on the legs of her slacks, she took a deep breath and tried to calm the jumble of anxiety tightening her stomach.

She was his mistress, she reminded herself as brutally

as she could. Not his girlfriend, not his fiancée, not even, really, his lover. This might be his family, but to her, they were simply another group of strangers she needed to entertain and impress to fulfill her part of the bargain.

Chase met her at the front of the car, only steps from the narrow porch that ran the full length of the front of the house.

"Ready?" he asked, seeming to sense her reluctance, even though she was doing her best to tame it.

She swallowed hard and let him take her hand, pasting on a wide smile she didn't quite feel. "Of course."

He led her onto the porch and through the front door. Voices assaulted them as soon as they stepped into the house. Male and female, one on top of the other.

They moved through a wide, homey living room that took up the front of the house, and down a short hallway that opened into a dining room filled with people—the source of all the noise.

Two men sat at one end of a long pine table already set with plates and silverware. One was older, one younger, but Elena could tell right away that they were related. Chase's father and brother, she would guess.

Beside the younger man stood a high chair with a brown-haired little girl seated inside, seemingly content to occupy herself by chewing on the wrong end of a small plastic spoon.

While Elena was taking in her surroundings, a swinging door opened and two women came out, both carrying a bowl or platter in each hand as they smiled and chatted.

"Chase!" the older of the two cried the moment she spotted them standing there. She quickly set sliced pot roast and buttered green beans on the table, then rushed toward them.

"Hi, Mom," Chase said, returning the woman's hug as she threw her arms around him and squeezed.

When they separated, his mother turned to face Elena. "And you must be Elena. Chase told us he might bring you along."

Elena returned her greeting and shook the woman's hand when she offered it, with Chase adding to the introduction.

"Elena, this is my mother, Theresa. And this is everyone else," he said, pointing as he went around the room. "My father, Isaac; my brother, Mitch; his wife, Emma; and their daughter, Amelia. Everyone, this is Elena Sanchez."

They all smiled and said hello, and she felt her anxiety begin to ease as Chase pulled out a chair and waited for her to take a seat, then sat down beside her.

Pot roast, mashed potatoes, green beans and sliced peaches were passed around the table, the room filling once again with noise as everyone started speaking at the same time. Voices and laughter mixing, conversations overlapping and turning on a dime.

Instead of being overwhelmed, Elena found the exuberant atmosphere comforting. It reminded her of some of her own family's gatherings, back before her mother died. She, Alandra and their father still ate meals together as often as possible, but they tended to be quieter, more subdued affairs these days.

Although she didn't take a large part in the interaction, she responded whenever questions were directed at her and found herself laughing several times at one thing or another. And as if the meal itself wasn't delicious enough, Theresa brought out a fresh-from-the-oven pecan pie that nearly made Elena weep.

With everyone stuffed, and little Amelia's eyes drooping, things began to quiet down. Elena helped Theresa clear the table and fill the dishwasher while Emma took the toddler upstairs to sleep and the men moved from the dining room to the living room. A few minutes later, they heard the front door open and then close, and Theresa rolled her eyes.

"Isaac thinks I don't know about those filthy cigars he likes to sneak after dinner. Like I can't smell them on him for hours afterward."

She reached into a cupboard and removed three short-stemmed wineglasses to go with the bottle of chardonnay she'd already set on the counter. Holding the three glasses upside down in one hand and the neck of the bottle in the other, she nudged the kitchen door with her hip and led the way through the house to the sitting room.

"He takes the boys outside with him so he can claim they needed to talk. I won't say anything tonight, though, since it will give us girls a chance to chat, too."

Emma came back downstairs then, to curl up in one corner of the overstuffed sofa. She smiled and thanked Theresa when the older woman passed her a half-full glass of wine.

Elena took a seat on the other end of the sofa, not quite at ease enough to put her feet up. But then, she was a guest here, not a daughter-in-law.

Theresa handed her a glass, too, then sat back in a matching armchair to sip from her own.

"So," Theresa murmured casually, "tell us how you came to be dating my son."

"So what's up with the raven-haired beauty?" Mitch asked, sipping at the three fingers of scotch he'd poured before their father had dragged them outside so he could sneak a few puffs from his cigar before their mother discovered him.

Chase took a sip from his own glass before responding. "Nothing's up. She's a friend, that's all."

"Mm-hmm." Keeping his gaze on the barn and paddock several yards from the house, his brother said, "You haven't brought a woman home to meet Mom and Dad since we were in high school."

"She seems like a nice girl," Isaac put in from farther down the porch railing. "I like her."

Chase elected not to respond to that. Mitch was right about him not bringing a girl home to meet his parents since they were both teenagers, but he didn't want to give anyone ideas.

He couldn't even say for sure why he'd brought Elena along tonight. It wasn't to meet his parents—not to see how she acted around them or what they thought of her.

He'd just…wanted company. He hadn't wanted to show up for yet another family dinner by himself, feeling a bit like an outsider now that his brother was married and so obviously happy with his wife and daughter. Ever since Mitch and Emma had gotten together, his parents—or at least his mother—had focused on seeing him settled down.

She wasn't single-minded about it, thank goodness. Only the occasional question about his personal life or remark about his finding a "good woman" to let him know he was still on her radar.

He'd known that even before asking Elena to accompany him tonight. So why the hell had he gone through with it, anyway?

Because it was part of their agreement. She would go with him to meetings and dinners whenever he needed her, and he'd needed someone with him tonight.

That's all there was to it, nothing more. The fact that his mother and father—and even his brother, apparently—were reading more into it was none of his concern.

Not that he hadn't noticed how well she fit in with the rowdy bunch he called family. She hadn't been overwhelmed by them, as he'd feared. Instead, she'd seemed to enjoy the boisterous camaraderie and had handled the many switches in conversation with ease.

Then again, what did he expect? Ever since he'd started spending time with her again, there wasn't a situation he could think of where she'd been uncomfortable or out of place.

Perhaps he'd been testing her, tossing her into the middle of one of his family's dinner gatherings to see if there was *anything* that caught her off guard. Or maybe he'd simply wanted her with him, wanted to share a part of his life with her that he hadn't before.

Of course, it didn't make him too happy to think that might be the case. If it was, he was in trouble. She was supposed to be his mistress…and only that because he wanted to exact a bit of revenge on her for the way she'd treated him in junior high.

A man didn't usually bring his mistress home to meet his parents. And a man bent on revenge certainly didn't look for ways to incorporate the subject of his vengeance more firmly into his life.

He threw back the last of his scotch at the same time his father stubbed out his cigar.

"She's just a friend," Chase repeated, his tone leaving no room for argument. Heading for the front door, he stopped with his hand on the knob to turn back and fix his brother with a warning glare. "Leave it alone."

As interrogations went, Elena supposed the one with Chase's mother and sister-in-law wasn't so bad. It had started with, "So, tell me how you came to be dating my son," but hadn't gone much farther than that.

Elena had explained that she wasn't dating Chase, that they were really just friends and business acquaintances. And Theresa Ramsey was savvy enough to realize her son wasn't a topic Elena cared to discuss, so she'd quickly moved into less personal, less dangerous territory.

They'd talked about Chase's and her trip to Vegas, but only in the vaguest of terms. About Chase's company, Ramsey Corporation, and how he'd built it from the ground up all on his own. About Elena's family—but again, only in the vaguest of terms—since Elena didn't particularly want to remind Theresa of the Christmas party they had attended where she had been so rude and cruel to Chase. And finally, about how Emma and Mitch had met—as children—and then ended up falling in love and getting married so many years later.

It was a lovely story, one that brought tears to Elena's eyes. For a moment, it almost made her believe true love existed and that fate could take a hand in a person's life, even if things had gotten off to a rocky start.

But what was she thinking? That some unseen force would reach down and bring her and Chase together?

Who was she trying to kid? Even if he found her physically irresistible…even if their current relationship lasted much longer than originally intended…she didn't think he would ever be able to get past what she'd done to him all those years ago.

She didn't blame him, but she did wish things could be different.

If only she hadn't been such a spoiled, arrogant brat as a teenager.

If only they had met again as adults with clean slates and no ugly baggage from their pasts.

Then, maybe they would have actually had a shot at making things work.

But the way it stood now, she knew they didn't. She also knew that when the time came for them to call it quits, a little part of her heart would break off and travel with him wherever he went.

Her chest tightened and her eyes began to dampen again. She quickly swallowed and took a deep breath, hoping her companions wouldn't notice the sudden rush of emotion that threatened to close her throat.

To her left, the front door creaked open and she welcomed the sudden distraction as Chase entered the room, followed by his brother and father.

Chase, she noticed, was carrying an empty tumbler and moved directly to the bar. For a moment, he hesitated, apparently contemplating a refill. But then he set his glass down and walked away.

Moving to the sofa, he took a seat at her side while his brother did the same beside his wife, so that the two women were at the ends with the two men sandwiched between them.

Rather than sit down, Isaac took up position behind his wife's chair. Close enough, Elena noticed, to play the part of the loving husband, but far enough away that Theresa wasn't likely to comment if she noticed the scent of cigar smoke lingering on his breath or clothes. To cover her grin, Elena lifted a hand to her mouth and pretended to cough.

For the next half hour, the six of them made small talk. Thankfully, the conversation completely avoided the topic of Chase's and her relationship.

And then it was time to leave. Chase stood, holding a hand out to her to help her to her feet, and everyone else followed suit.

Theresa and Emma both hugged Elena while Isaac and Mitch shook her hand and wished her well. She was invited to come back any time, and she promised that she would, even though she suspected such an event would never actually take place.

In the car, Elena waited until Chase had started the engine and turned down the driveway before leaning against the headrest and releasing a long breath. The bright headlights created twin streaks of yellow along the dirt lane.

"Tired?" Chase asked, glancing in her direction before returning his attention to the road.

"Not really," she answered honestly. She was, but only because she'd been so nervous and tense about meeting his family to begin with. With the anxiety behind her, she suddenly felt like a blown-up balloon pricked by a pin and allowed to expel its air all at once. "I was just thinking about how nice your family is. Thank you for introducing them to me."

A beat of heavy silence passed, then he said, "They liked you, too."

She smiled in the darkness. "I'm glad."

He turned on the radio and the soft strains of a classical CD filled the space around them. Neither of them spoke another word until they neared her house.

At a stop sign, Chase stopped. Only when they remained there for longer than Elena thought was necessary did she look at him, brows drawn together in an unspoken query. His fingers flexed on the steering wheel and he didn't meet her gaze.

"I can take you home," he said slowly. "Or you can come back to my place with me."

Her stomach jumped and every inch of her skin broke out in gooseflesh, tingling as though she'd just been touched by a live wire.

She licked her lips, her mouth gone dry. "I…can go home with you, I guess," she told him in a soft voice.

His only response was a tight nod. Then, instead of turning right as he would have to drop her off, he went straight, toward his own home.

She'd never given much thought to where he lived. Whenever she pictured him in his own environment, it was his office, behind his desk, as he'd been that first time she'd gone to plead her father's case. Aside from that, she supposed she'd always assumed he lived in an apartment somewhere, perhaps a penthouse on the top floor of the Ramsey Corporation office building.

A man like Chase—single, wealthy, independent— wouldn't need much space. Just a bedroom, bathroom, small kitchen and of course an office where he could work.

So her jaw nearly dropped when he turned into an upscale housing development and stopped in the driveway of a gorgeous, sprawling two-story brick home.

"This is your house?" she asked as he cut the engine, not bothering to hide her awe.

He sat back in his seat, offering a wry smile. "Yeah, why? Did you think I lived at some cheap hotel? Or maybe sleep at my desk at work?"

She flushed at just how close his guess was to what she'd been thinking and was glad it was too dark for him to see.

"No," she denied, "I just didn't realize you owned your own house. It's gorgeous."

"Thank you. Though it's not quite the mansion you grew up in, I know."

He opened his door and stepped out and she followed suit.

"Yes, well, even I admit Pop went a bit overboard when he built it. He was the first member of his family to really make something of himself, and I think he confused the house from *Gone with the Wind* with the average American dream."

That earned her a chuckle and she joined in as he led her up the moonlit path to the front door. Reaching around the jamb, he flipped a switch. Light flooded the foyer and part of the front yard from a massive chandelier hanging in the center of the ceiling where dozens of crystal teardrops twinkled brightly.

"Would you like a tour?"

She nodded eagerly, already fascinated by the little she'd seen.

He showed her the den, kitchen and family room, and stood in front of a set of wide French doors at the back of the house as he described the patio and lawn that she couldn't see much of in the muted illumination from the house. There was also an indoor pool and workout room, two things even her father's sizeable estate couldn't boast.

Then he led her upstairs and pointed out several beautifully decorated guest rooms, as well as a central restroom that didn't look as though it was used very often.

At the end of the hall stood the master bedroom, easily twice as large as any of the others, and done in dark, masculine tones. The bed was a giant four poster made of mahogany and covered with a comforter of forest green and navy blue swirls. On either side of the bed stood two-drawer nightstands carved of the same wood and with the same design as the bedposts, and holding matching wrought iron lamps. A doorway to the right of the bed led to the master bath, with a sunken whirlpool tub, a separate shower and two sinks set into a long marble countertop.

As though she wasn't impressed enough already, he informed her that he'd overseen both the design and decoration of the entire house. The man had great taste, she admitted, more than a little surprised by just how luxurious and tasteful his home was.

It was a shame, though, that he lived there alone. Such a large place seemed wasted on only one person.

"So," he murmured, "would you like a glass of wine, or something else to drink?"

They were still standing in the middle of the bedroom, but while she had felt completely comfortable a moment ago, she was suddenly faced with an attack of nerves. Her reason for being in his home, alone with him, this late at night flashed back to her and her heart gave a tiny flip.

"No, thank you," she said softly with a shake of her head. She'd had two glasses of chardonnay at his parents' house. Any more and her head might start to get fuzzy.

Her fingers worked distractedly on the strap of her purse as she added, "I should call my sister, though. Let her know I'm going to be late."

He nodded, then pointed to the cordless phone charging on one of the nightstands. "Help yourself."

Striding to the walk-in closet at the far side of the room, he shrugged out of his suit jacket and hung it in the jungle of other suit jackets.

"If you'd like," he said as she was dialing, "you can tell her I'll bring you home in the morning." Cocking his head in her direction, he shot her a glance filled with sultry and seductive meaning. "That is, if you'd like to stay the night."

Ten

Elena inhaled deeply and stretched, her toes curling into the soft Egyptian cotton sheets, her arms reaching over her head until her fingers bumped the mahogany headboard.

She couldn't remember the last time she'd slept so well. Of course, she and Chase had worn themselves out pretty well before finally drifting off sometime after midnight.

At the sound of movement in the room, she opened her eyes and sat up, clutching the covers to her chest. Chase wasn't beside her in the gigantic four poster bed, but already up and dressed. With a tray in his hands, he crossed the carpeted floor in bare feet, well-worn jeans and a casual white button-down shirt with the sleeves rolled to his elbows.

The tray held a plate piled high with what looked like French toast and scrambled eggs, two glasses of orange juice and a tall, narrow vase with a single bright purple tulip in full bloom.

"Good morning," he said, his low drawl dripping down her spine like warm honey.

"Good morning," she returned as he rounded the bed and crawled onto the mattress from his side, setting the tray carefully between them. It looked and smelled delicious.

"What time is it?" she asked, turning her head toward the clock on the bedside table.

Before she could see for herself, he said, "A little after nine."

"Nine?" Shock and fear rolled through her as she realized she was late for work. She was never late for work.

She threw back the covers, ready to jump out of bed and dress as quickly as possible. If she hurried, maybe she could get to the office before her boss realized she was late, even if it meant showing up in the same outfit two days in a row.

She would rather put up with gossip about her personal life than gain the reputation of shirking her duties. And if she called Alandra from her cell phone on the way, she might even be able to get her sister to meet her there with a change of clothes.

"Relax," Chase told her, reaching out to grab her wrist before she'd leapt completely off the mattress. "I phoned your sister and asked her to call you in sick from work."

For a moment, Elena wasn't sure she understood what he was telling her. Then, as it began to sink in, she raised a curious brow.

"Although, if you'd like to leave the covers off and eat in the buff," he added with a devilish wink, "I'm all for it."

She looked down and saw that she was, indeed, naked,

the sheet tossed off to her ankles. With a gasp, she grabbed the sheet and yanked it back up to her chin.

He chuckled at the blush that filled her cheeks. "Do you really think there's any part of you I haven't already seen?" he asked, and then added, "And explored quite thoroughly?"

It was true. He was a very thorough man.

"I don't make a habit of sitting around, eating breakfast in the nude," she replied primly, turning her nose up just a little.

Which only earned her another deep laugh.

"And what do you mean you asked my sister to call me in sick to work?" she demanded, pretending to be more annoyed than she really was.

In all honestly, she was relieved. Yes, it was highhanded of him, but then, this was Chase. Chase was nothing if not forceful and commanding.

He shrugged one broad shoulder. "I kept you up pretty late last night, so I figured you'd appreciate a morning to sleep in. I also thought we could spend the day together, since I called and let my secretary know I wouldn't be in, either."

Now, that surprised her. She didn't think Chase Ramsey ever took a day off work, or would know what to do with himself if he did.

Since it seemed like a moot point now, she gave up on worrying about her job and reached for a fork and the plate of French toast.

"What did you have in mind?" she asked.

"Hey, that's for both of us," he complained when she dug in.

"I'll let you have whatever I can't finish," she shot back with a wicked tip to her lips.

He snorted, but let her go. Then he said, "We can do anything you like. Sit by the pool sipping umbrella drinks, or on the back patio doing the same. We can even pack a picnic lunch and go over to my brother's to see if he'll let us take a couple of his horses out for a few hours."

For a man who professed to need her only as his mistress, he seemed awfully accommodating all of a sudden. A picnic lunch? Sipping umbrella drinks by the pool?

She took a bite of French toast and chewed slowly, then washed it down with a sip of juice.

As much as she enjoyed horseback riding, the thought of staying here and spending the day only with Chase held much more appeal. After all, she didn't know how much longer they would have together before he decided he didn't need a mistress anymore…or at least didn't need *her* as his mistress.

"A dip in the pool sounds like fun," she said slowly. "I don't have a suit, though."

"That's all right." He reached out and snagged a slice of French toast from the plate she was holding and lifted it directly to his mouth. "You don't need one."

"You expect me to swim naked?" she asked, somewhat startled.

"Why not?" He took another bite, chewing thoughtfully. "I'll be naked, too, and even if you did wear a suit, I'd have you out of it in no time, anyway."

She paused with the fork almost to her mouth, her throat closing suddenly as a jolt of arousal flushed through her system. Lowering her hand, she replaced the fork on the plate and set it all aside. Chase didn't miss a beat in picking it up himself and digging in.

"What do you say?" he asked, mouth half-full of food. "Do you still want to swim?"

The vision of frolicking in the water with him, making love with him there, flashed through her head, and the muscles in her body went lax. She swallowed hard, licked her dry lips and barely managed a breathless, "Okay."

Hours later, Elena was glad she hadn't had to go to work that day. She wasn't sure she'd have the energy to even go in tomorrow.

Chase was stretched out on a lounge chair a few feet from the pool, eyes closed, chest rising and falling with his breathing. She was draped along his side, her head on his shoulder, her palm resting on the flat of his abdomen. And they were both entirely, blissfully naked.

Two colorful drinks, complete with the umbrellas he'd promised, sat on a small glass table beside the chair, practically untouched, and soft music played over the sound system that was piped through the entire house.

"I've got a party to attend tomorrow night," he said, startling her out of her drowsy reverie.

Rolling her head back slightly, she realized his eyes were still closed, but he obviously wasn't asleep as she'd first thought.

"You wanna go with me?"

"Do I have a choice?" she asked, shifting slightly to re-distribute her weight along his chest and thigh.

"You always have a choice. We all do," he replied calmly. Lifting his arm, he thread his fingers through the damp hair at her temple. "But I'm asking you. It's a business gathering, but you don't have to go if you don't want to. I can make it through one black-tie party on my own, I think," he added with a chuckle.

She felt his laughter vibrate through his body, and nearly sighed at the tender, relaxing sensation he was creating along her scalp.

"I'd like you with me, though, if you'd like to go."

Swallowing hard, she tried not to let her emotions tense her muscles or hasten her breathing, but her mind was spinning.

Was this a turning point in their relationship? Was he beginning to see her more as a lover, a girlfriend, than simply a mistress by business arrangement?

She didn't want to get her hopes up, didn't want to read too much into his one small comment, his one tiny shift in attitude. But her heart swelled with the possibilities.

"I would like to," she said softly, relieved when her voice came out steady and self-assured.

"Good. I'll pick you up at eight."

Then, without warning, he rolled over, twisting her beneath him, catching her just before she fell off the edge of the chaise. She gave a little yelp, her eyes going wide in startlement.

"Wear something slinky and sexy that shows off your great breasts and bottom."

He pinched her there and she made a sound that was half-gasp, half-laugh.

"You think I have a nice bottom?" she asked when she'd regained her breath.

"Stellar. Classic. Greek statues weep in envy."

She grinned, letting her head fall back as he nuzzled her throat. His unshaven cheek scratched along her tender flesh, likely leaving a mark that she would later have to explain to her family and co-workers, but she didn't care. Her back arched in pleasure, her hips bumping into his obvious arousal.

His hands slid higher as his mouth moved to her ear. "And make sure it's backless. Something that leaves your smooth, gorgeous back bare to the room. Every other woman there will want to scratch your eyes out," he murmured. "And every man will want you."

"Including you?" she asked, finally getting into the flow of his building passion. She lifted her arms around his neck, her legs around his waist and licked the line of his jaw.

"Especially me. I'll be wanting you even before I pick you up."

He emphasized his point by slipping inside her in one long, steady stroke. Her lungs seized, and for the rest of the afternoon, all the thoughts and concerns jumbling through her mind were pushed aside by the sinful, delicious things Chase did to her.

Ever an agreeable mistress, Elena wore something slinky, sexy and backless that she hoped did an adequate job of highlighting her chest and rear. Chase, she supposed, would be the judge of that.

She couldn't wait to see his reaction when he caught his first glimpse of her. He would be there any minute, and all she had left to do was slip on her necklace and earrings.

Her gown was red and floor-length, with a slit that ran to mid-thigh. The material was struck through with silver threads so that every bit of it shimmered, especially when she moved. The bodice, cut in a deep vee and tied behind her neck, left her shoulders and back completely bare.

She wore high, red heels with a criss-cross design across the top of her foot. Tiny rhinestones sparkled at the junction where each of the straps crossed.

Her jewelry was surprisingly simple—just a diamond pendant at her neck, matching teardrop earrings and an understated tennis bracelet on her right wrist.

According to Alandra, she looked "hot enough to peel the paint off a '57 Mustang." Whatever that meant. But she'd laughed anyway, and taken it as the compliment she was sure her sister meant it to be.

Grabbing her small red clutch, she left her bedroom and headed downstairs. Her foot had just cleared the last step when the doorbell rang. She moved across the foyer, her high heels clicking on the polished parquet floor, and opened the door.

The sun was beginning to set, but it was still light enough to make out every detail of Chase's broad, masculine form. And that form was positively mouthwatering in a tuxedo.

His black hair was slicked back instead of being left in its usual, carefree style, making him look sexier and more sophisticated.

She started to lick her lips, then remembered the recently applied lipstick and forced herself to rein in her roving tongue.

"Wow," he muttered, reading her mind. "You look fabulous."

"Thank you," she said, then did a little pirouette in the doorway. "Does my dress meet with your approval? It's slinky, sexy, shows off my breasts and bottom and is even—" She turned again, flashing the expanse of her back, left completely bare by both the dress and her upswept hair. "—backless."

"Nice. Very nice," he drawled. Reaching out, he ran the knuckle of one index finger along her spine, from the small of her back to the nape of her neck.

She shivered, both from his touch and the low, suggestive tone. If she wasn't careful, they would end up rolling around on the floor of her father's entryway and miss the party altogether.

Slowly, she turned around to face him, placing her hand on her stomach in an attempt to quell the butterflies swooping and swirling inside.

"Should we go?" she asked.

With a heartfelt sigh, he hung his head and let his arm fall back to his side. "If we must."

She smiled, following him onto the front stoop and closing the door behind her.

He helped her into the car, then walked around and took a seat on the driver's side.

It took nearly half an hour to reach the hotel where the fund-raiser was being held. When they arrived, Chase passed his keys to the valet before rounding the hood, opening her door and taking her hand as she stepped out.

With her arm linked at his elbow, they strode through the luxurious hotel's lobby, took the elevator to the fourth floor and crossed to the entrance of the decorated, already packed ballroom. For a minute, they stood at the open double doors, taking in their surroundings.

Just before Chase took a step to lead her inside, Elena tipped her head and glanced up to meet his gaze.

"Oh, I almost forgot," she said in as innocent a tone as she could muster. Then she stood up on tiptoe and leaned close to his ear to whisper, "I'm not wearing panties."

I'm not wearing panties.
I'm not wearing panties.
I'm not wearing panties.

The ballroom was crowded with people, most of whom he knew, many of whom he'd done business with. A hundred voices mingled together, raising the volume to near headache level.

And still, all he heard was those four words Elena had whispered in his ear a split second before they'd stepped into the party.

Stepped. Yeah, right. He'd been so stunned by her erotic admission that he'd been frozen in place. Riveted to the spot, his entire body hot and flaring like a lit match tip with unleashed passion. She'd had to practically drag him the rest of the way into the room. He couldn't have taken a single step on his own if his life depended on it.

And, frankly, he hadn't wanted to. The last thing he'd wanted to do at that point was mingle with business acquaintances and make small talk all night. He'd have rather written a sizeable check to tonight's charity—whatever the heck it was, anyway—and dragged Elena off to the nearest bed. His, hers, one of the hotel's…he honestly didn't care.

But even though she'd prodded him to do the right thing and go through with his plans for the evening, he heard nothing but her voice echoing in his brain.

I'm not wearing panties.

His gaze slipped—not for the first time—to her rear end, which swayed beneath the slithery, shimmery material of her gown when she moved.

If she hadn't told him she was naked beneath, would he have figured it out on his own?

Maybe. Lord knows he's spent his fair share of time staring at her derriere.

Then again, probably not. It wasn't like he was an expert on women's underwear or panty-lines.

But now that he knew…man, now that he knew, he couldn't seem to concentrate on anything else.

People kept coming up to him, Elena kept pulling him from place to place to chat, and he didn't think he'd heard a word any of them had said. She'd thoroughly scrambled his brain and sent every ounce of blood in his body just below the equator.

"Can we leave yet?" he whispered in her ear the first chance he got, pressing himself along her back so she would know exactly *why* he wanted to get out of there.

With a wide smile on her face for everyone else's benefit, she cocked her head in his direction and said, "We just got here. It would be rude to leave so soon."

He took the plate she offered, covered with a little bit of everything from the dinner buffet, while she turned back to get something for herself.

Leaning close, he let his breath stir the hair at her nape. "Then let's find a dark corner somewhere so we can be alone."

She laughed, the sweet tinkling sound going straight to his gut. His fingers clenched so tightly on the plate in his hand, he was surprised it didn't shatter.

"I'm not going to sneak off with you in the middle of this event so you can have your wicked way with me."

Her voice was moderately chastising, but her eyes glimmered with a sensual, teasing light.

"Then you shouldn't have told me about your underwear," he growled.

She blinked a couple of times with supreme innocence, then replied with equal innocence, "But I'm not wearing any."

His teeth snapped together hard enough to crack his molars. "That's what I mean," he hissed through tight lips.

With both their plates filled, she sashayed away from the buffet and toward the large round table where they'd been assigned seats with three other couples he recognized, but barely knew. Chase had no choice but to follow. When they reached the table, Elena set her plate at her place, then took his and did the same.

Still with that overly bright smile on her face, she moved close to him and whispered, "That was just an aperitif. A tiny treat to keep you interested until this little soiree is over, when we can go back to your place and do all of the things I know you're fantasizing about right now."

He studied her for a minute, nostrils flaring as he breathed heavily through his nose. She had no idea how close she was coming to being thrown over his shoulder and hauled out of there like a sack of grain. It would cause a horrified uproar, and their pictures would probably be in the morning paper, but at this point he honestly didn't care.

Then she moved even closer, brushing against him from shoulder to thigh as she took her seat from the side closest to him rather than farthest away.

"I promise it will be worth the wait," she murmured softly before sitting down.

Rather than tempering the desire that thrummed through his veins, her words threw fuel on the fire. But there was something to be said for waiting, wanting, letting arousal build to a near-agonizing level.

And when he finally got her alone, he would hold her to her promise. There were at least sixteen highly evocative images simmering in his brain at this very moment, and he intended to make sure they executed every single one.

He pulled out his own chair and sat down, muttering for her ears only, "It better be."

She smiled at his attempt to pout and patted his knee.

For the next hour, they picked at their meals, sipped champagne and chatted with the people around them. Chase couldn't have cared less about what anyone was saying, but he was well-schooled in the art of schmoozing.

After the food and drink and requisite speeches, everyone got up from their seats and once again began to mingle. This was when he could lean in and say, *We're out of here,* and drag her off the way he'd been dying to all night.

He put his hand on her elbow, prepared to do exactly that, when a small gaggle of tall, willowy, attractive women sidled up to them, their gazes sweeping over him before settling on Elena.

"Elena?" one in a low-cut lavender gown queried. "Elena Sanchez?"

"Yes?" Elena returned, her eyes warm and welcoming, as they'd been all night. Chase was beginning to think of it as her "polite public demeanor," the way she interacted with everyone from his business associates, to the chairwoman of tonight's fund-raiser, to the servers who milled around clearing tables and making sure no one's glass ever became truly empty.

"I thought it was you," the other woman practically squealed, taking Elena's hands in both of her own and giving them a squeeze. "I haven't seen you in years. Since high school."

The other three women in the little clique nodded and smiled just as widely. But when Elena didn't seem to recognize them, the one in lavender clucked her tongue and gave her an admonishing eye roll.

"Tisha Ferguson. We went to school together. Of course, I'm Mrs. Ferguson-McDonald now." She waved her left hand, making sure everyone in a six-foot radius got a glimpse of the huge diamond weighing down her ring finger. "I married very, very well."

To keep from scoffing Chase tightened his jaw until the bones nearly cracked. She'd married well. Well, bully for her. So had every other woman present. A person couldn't spit in this room without hitting a woman who had married very, *very* well.

"Tisha!" Elena said. "Of course. You look wonderful, I barely recognized you."

Leaning in, the two women kissed—that double cheek thing Chase had never understood. Then Elena's glance slid to the other women standing just behind Tisha.

"Leslie. Stephanie. Candy. It's nice to see you again. How have you been?"

The five of them chatted for a few minutes, with Tisha—the obvious spokesperson for the group—monopolizing most of the conversation. Finally, when there was an opening, Elena turned to him and attempted introductions.

"Do you remember Chase Ramsey?" she asked the four of them. "He went to school with us, too, though he was a year or two ahead of us."

The three standing back a bit smiled and nodded, but Tisha tipped her head and studied him more closely through narrowed, heavily painted eyes.

"Chase Ramsey. You're not..." Her glossy pink lips, previously pursed in thought, widened a split second before she broke into a high-pitched, cackling laugh. "Oh, my God! Chase Ramsey. I remember you now. You're that pathetic farmer's son who asked Elena to dance at that Christmas party at her parents' house. You should have seen your face when she turned you down. Oh, it was priceless!"

Eleven

Tisha threw back her head and chortled loudly, the other three joining in on a slightly less obnoxious scale.

Elena felt her heartbeat accelerate and a cold skittering of foreboding snake down her spine. The fingers of both hands curled instinctively as she fought the urge to plow her fist into the stuck-up witch's face.

Horrified, she glanced at Chase and saw the fury spark in his eyes before a mask of indifference dropped into place, hiding his true feelings from the world.

"Chase," she began, desperate to hold on to him. But before she'd even finished breathing his name, he turned on his heel and stalked away.

As she stared at his back, Tisha's laughter grew in both volume and venom.

And suddenly, Elena couldn't take it anymore. She

spun on her former friend, just keeping from reaching out to slap the smug grin off her face.

"How dare you," Elena charged.

Leslie, Stephanie and Candy quieted immediately, their mouths rolling into tiny Os of surprise that anyone would dare speak to their queen in such a tone. It took a moment longer for Tisha to settle, but finally the gleeful expression washed from her face and her eyes narrowed in annoyance.

"Excuse me?" she responded haughtily.

"What gives you the right to talk to people like that? To treat them like they're beneath you?"

Tisha's nose began to tip up, but Elena plowed ahead, not caring a whit that their confrontation was starting to draw a crowd.

"Do you know what you are, Tisha? You're a bitch. An arrogant, selfish, snobbish *bitch*. I'm sorry I ever met you, let alone was a part of your vicious little pack of hyenas back in high school."

Her blood was boiling, her lungs burning with the effort to suck in enough air for all she had to say to this woman.

"*You're* the one who's pathetic, Tisha Ferguson-McDonald." She sneered the hyphenated last name, making it as much of an insult as she could manage. "*You're* the one who should be embarrassed by your up-bringing, your appearance, your very existence, because you aren't half the human being Chase Ramsey is. He's the one who should be looking down his nose at you, not the other way around."

There was so much more she was feeling, so much more she wanted to say, but none of it was worth the time she was losing in following Chase.

Leaving Tisha and her cohorts with their mouths hanging open in shock, she spun around and pushed her way through the crowd, following the path Chase had taken only moments ago. The closer she got to the doors of the ballroom, the faster she moved until she was all but running.

Through the crowd, through the open double doors. In the spacious hallway, she stopped, looked around, but didn't see him.

Racing to the elevator, she elbowed people aside and pushed the down button, punching it over and over again until the doors closed and the compartment began to move.

"Come on, come on," she muttered, wishing belatedly that she had taken the stairs. Even in heels, she was convinced she could have made it to the lobby faster than the elevator was doing the job.

When the doors opened, she burst out, hurrying across the marble floor, glancing right and left for any sign of him. Outside, she scanned the cars coming and going, being both brought up and taken away by the crew of valets. Rushing up to the nearest green-vested worker, she described Chase and his car, and asked if the man had seen him.

"Oh, yeah," the man said, pointing toward the end of the hotel's long, curved driveway. "He just took off."

Elena's gaze followed the direction of the valet's finger. She saw brake lights flash for an instant and then tires squealed as the driver pulled away.

There was no use running after him, no use trying to catch up. He was gone, and Elena didn't know if she would ever get him back.

* * *

It had been two days since the party. Two days since Chase had taken off. Two days he'd refused to speak to her.

She'd taken a taxi to his house straight from the hotel, but either he hadn't gone home, or he simply hadn't answered the doorbell or her desperate knocking.

Although it was the last thing she wanted to do, she'd gone home from there and immediately tried to call him. First at home, then on his cell and even at his office. There'd been no answer, and he hadn't bothered to call her back, even though she'd continued to call several times a day, leaving numerous messages.

Elena suspected he was at work, but whenever she called, his receptionist asked for her name, then quickly told her he was unavailable.

He wasn't unavailable. He was avoiding her, and she knew it.

She could just strangle Tisha Ferguson-McDonald for her rudeness and insensitivity. Forty-eight hours later, she still wanted to track the woman down and slap her silly.

But most of all, she wanted to apologize to Chase and make sure he was all right. Well, he wasn't all right, as she was well aware. Otherwise he wouldn't have stormed out of the charity event, leaving her to find her own way home, and he wouldn't be dodging her calls.

Still, she felt she owed him an explanation, owed it to him to let him know she hadn't stood around and joined in on Tisha's cruel laughter and remarks after he'd left. She'd been a fool to be friends with those girls as a teenager, but she wasn't a fool any longer.

She'd also learned—possibly the hard way—just what

kind of man Chase Ramsey was, and that if she'd been smart, she would have danced with him that night at her parents' Christmas party and left her so-called friends standing there feeling stupid and alone.

Even if he couldn't forgive her, even if Tisha's careless comments had brought back too many old feelings, opened too many old wounds, she needed him to know *she* wasn't like that anymore.

When the phone on her desk rang, she froze, her heart dropping to her stomach. She hadn't been getting much work done, anyway, between praying Chase would call and her many attempts to call him, but she was almost afraid to answer for fear it *wouldn't* be him.

Finally, after four rings, she took a deep breath and picked up the receiver.

"Elena Sanchez," she answered, as she always did her work phone.

"Miss Sanchez, this is Nancy, Chase Ramsey's personal assistant. Mr. Ramsey would like you to meet him this evening at Chez Pierre at seven o'clock. You'll be accompanying him to a business dinner, so please dress appropriately."

Elena went from disappointed, when she realized the caller wasn't Chase, to surprised at the woman's words. With the fast-paced, matter-of-fact delivery, it took a moment for the request to sink in.

"Do you have any questions about these instructions, Miss Sanchez?" the woman prodded.

"No. I mean, yes! Yes." Elena was leaning forward on her desk, her free hand squeezing the phone cord so tightly, she was amazed the reception remained clear. "Is Chase there? Can I please talk to him?"

"I'm sorry," his assistant apologized with a distinct lack of emotion, "Mr. Ramsey isn't available at the moment, but he will see you tonight at Chez Pierre. Don't be late."

And then the line went dead, leaving Elena feeling empty and confused.

He wanted her to meet him tonight for a business dinner. What did that mean? Had he forgiven her for whatever imagined slight she'd committed the other night at the party? Had he gotten over Tisha's rude remarks?

And if so, why hadn't he called her himself? Why had his assistant contacted her and been so cold, when the woman had always been friendly to her before?

She didn't have answers to any of her questions and wouldn't until she saw him tonight. Only five more hours, she thought, glancing at her watch.

Five more hours until she would see Chase again, and could find out how he really felt about her.

From where he was sitting, Chase watched Elena enter the restaurant. She looked gorgeous, as always, in a brown and black animal print skirt and frothy brown blouse that dipped into a deep V in front.

But this time, he wasn't going to let her body or her smile affect him. He'd been crazy to ever let her get under his skin at all.

Convincing her to share his bed and accompany him to a few business dinners had been a bad idea to begin with. What had he been thinking?

Oh, he knew. He'd been thinking he could exact a little revenge for the way she'd treated him when they were kids, and get lucky in the process.

Hmph. Look how well that had turned out.

He took another gulp of the wine he'd been nursing since he'd arrived half an hour ago, glad Elena hadn't spotted him yet and made her way over. It was cruel of him, perhaps, but he wasn't going to lift a hand to draw her attention. He needed as much time as he could get before he had to be close to her again. Smelling her perfume and the fragrant shampoo she used on her hair…seeing her soft skin and remembering how it felt to touch, to stroke, to taste.

Against his will, his body hardened, every muscle going taut with desire.

Damn her. And damn his traitorous soul for still wanting her.

He didn't *want* to want her. He wanted to punish her—for what she'd done twenty years ago and for what had happened the other night.

His gaze narrowed as the rage began to roll through him. Rage, tempered with a modicum of embarrassment and a fair share of good old-fashioned lust.

She was coming toward him now, a tentative smile on her face. He could almost see her mind racing, wondering what she would encounter when she reached him.

Would he stand up, take her hand and kiss her cheek before inviting her to sit beside him? Or would he remain stoic and barely speak to her as she found her own place at the table to await their other guests?

He pushed aside the niggling of guilt that tried to convince him to forgive her, to let go of what had happened the other night at the fund-raiser and allow their relationship to fall back to the way it had been when she'd spent the night at his house. In his arms.

But that ship had definitely sailed and his head was once again on straight.

Elena was his mistress for as long as it took her father to get Sanchez Restaurant Supply back into the black—if he ever could—or until she decided to call things off. In which case, Chase would swoop in and buy out SRS, as originally planned.

But until one or the other of those things occurred, he intended to take full advantage of their arrangement.

She approached the table, still smiling, the maitre d' at her side, ready to hold her chair and see her properly seated beside Chase, leaving the other side open for the other two members of their party. Hiding her small purse beneath the cloth-covered table, she pulled her chair a fraction closer and nodded when the newly arrived waiter offered to fill her glass with the same dark claret Chase was drinking.

Her heart was pounding a mile a minute, and she was grinning so widely she was afraid her face would crack. Chase still hadn't spoken, which only made her stomach tighten all the more.

"Hi," she said brightly. So brightly, it hurt her own ears. She sounded like a puppet on one of those upbeat children's morning shows.

He nodded, taking a sip of his wine.

"I'm glad you called. Or at least had Nancy call for you," she added with a grin.

Leaning in, she lowered her voice and reached out to touch him. Before she could make contact, he once again raised his glass to his lips. She swallowed hard and drew back her hand.

It didn't mean anything, she told herself. Just because he hadn't spoken to her yet and apparently didn't welcome her touch didn't mean he was angry with her or still hurt about the other evening.

Maybe he simply wasn't a fan of participating in public displays of affection, however tame. Or maybe he was afraid his business associates would walk in any minute and get the wrong idea.

"I've been trying to reach you," she went on as though he wasn't acting the least bit peculiar. Folding her hands in her lap, she met his eyes. "Chase, I want to talk to you about—"

"Here they are," he said shortly, cutting her off. "This is a very important business associate and his wife. I'd appreciate if you'd be on your best behavior and try *not* to embarrass me."

Her eyes widened at his sharp warning. In all the time she'd been accompanying him to events and dinners like this one, she'd never done or said anything to embarrass him, nor had he ever felt the need to dictate her behavior before.

She found it more than a little strange. But maybe he was still smarting over Tisha's remarks. She couldn't blame him, and since she still felt she owed him an apology for that, she decided not to hold his apparently lousy mood against him.

He introduced her to the other couple, and Elena did her best to make witty, companionable small talk while they studied the menus, placed their orders and shared another glass of wine. While Chase was polite enough to Mr. and Mrs. Hasslebeck, he remained cold toward her. Which was why she jumped when his hand cupped her knee and started sliding upward.

The wine she was drinking sloshed against the sides of her glass and she gasped as it narrowly missed spilling on her blouse. Every eye at the table turned to her.

She laughed nervously, unnecessarily straightening the items at her place setting and jiggling her leg beneath the table in an attempt to shake off Chase's fingers. They didn't budge.

"I'm sorry," she apologized. "I was afraid I'd spilled wine on my clothes. You know how hard it is to get stains out of silk."

The other woman agreed with a chuckle and launched into a diatribe about some of the more stubborn stains she'd encountered in her lifetime.

Instead of being daunted by the turn in conversation or her attempt to dislodge his hand, Chase seemed even more determined to reach his goal. The hem of her skirt began to bunch as he roamed higher on her thigh.

His fingers skimmed between her legs and she had to bite her tongue to keep from making a sound. She clamped her thighs together, trapping his hand and stopping its maddening ascent.

Thankfully, their meals arrived a second later. He tugged and she reluctantly loosened her grip, knowing he needed his right hand to eat.

At least while he was busy at that, he wouldn't be feeling her up, she thought with distaste.

Not that she was opposed to Chase groping her under the right circumstances. She just didn't think they should be messing around beneath the tablecloth during what was supposed to be a business dinner. After warning her to be on *her* best behavior, shouldn't he be more careful of his own actions?

The meal passed without incident, and with Chase and
Mr. Hasslebeck spending a good deal of time discussing
business. Elena had just begun to breathe easy again when
the coffee and desserts arrived, only to feel that telltale
tickling once again.

Glancing over, she found Chase sipping his coffee,
which he held in his left hand. His right was beneath the
table…and crawling steadily upward.

"Excuse me," she said, pulling the cloth napkin from
her lap and setting it beside the small plate holding a delicious-looking chunk of tiramisu as she got to her feet.
"I'm just going to run to the restroom."

Without waiting for a response, she retrieved her
purse and headed for the rear of the restaurant. Once
inside the ladies' room, she rested her hands on the edge
of the counter and took several deep breaths, gazing at
her reflection in the mirror over the sinks. Behind her, a
stall door opened, and the only other person in the
restroom smiled as she walked up, washed and dried
her hands, then left.

As soon as the door closed behind the woman, Elena
shook herself, tore off a piece of paper towel, and wet it
with cold water, dabbing her chest, her forehead, the nape
of her neck.

She might not approve of what Chase had been trying
to do out there, but that didn't mean it had no effect on her.
One touch of his hand and she melted like snow on the first
day of spring. Even now her knees were as weak as cooked
noodles and her nerve endings were fluttering with unful-
filled desire.

The ladies' room door swung open again, and she

quickly straightened, pretending to be just finishing up so no one would think she'd been hiding...even if that's exactly what she was doing.

She smiled and turned to greet the woman who had entered on her way out. Her face fell when—instead of another woman—she found Chase leaning nonchalantly against the closed restroom door. His mouth curved with satisfaction, his eyes burning with devilish intent.

"What are you doing here?" she asked harshly, her fingers tightening on the damp paper towel in her hand.

Reaching behind him, he flipped the bolt on the main door, locking them inside, then took a menacing step forward. "What do you think?"

She took a step back, her hip bumping into the countertop. "You can't be in here," she told him in what she hoped was a stern voice. "This is the ladies' room."

He kept walking, leaning over to check for feet visible under the stall doors. Then, when he found them all empty, he straightened and turned his attention fully on her. "I know what it is. And I know what I want."

It was clear from his expression that what he wanted was her.

She'd never seen him like this before. Passionate, yes. Eager. Determined. But he'd also always maintained a sense of control that seemed to be missing at the moment. As many times as they'd made love, and as hot as they'd been for each other, he'd never been driven to lock them in a public bathroom and take her while guests—*his* guests—were waiting to finish their dessert.

"Chase..."

She held out her hand, even threw the balled-up paper

towel at his chest. He only chuckled and continued stalking forward, already loosening his belt buckle.

She twisted, intending to leap for the locked door, but he caught her, pulled her around and pushed her against the row of sinks.

"Chase, no. We can't."

"Oh, yes, we can." His mouth covered hers while his fingers made short work of his slacks and then moved to the bottom of her skirt. "We just have to be quick and quiet about it."

He lifted her enough to hike her skirt to her waist, then set her more fully on the counter. His thumbs hooked into the sides of her garter belt and panties, pulling the delicate garments down to her ankles with one swift yank. She thought she heard something tear, but couldn't find it in her to care.

She hardly had time to breathe, let alone think, as he pried her legs apart, then closed the short distance between them and filled her to overflowing.

She gasped, her fingers digging into his shoulders, her thighs clutching at him as tightly as they could from such an awkward angle. He thrust hard and fast, his mouth scouring her face and throat, his hands dancing over her breasts and spine and buttocks—anywhere he could reach.

Her hips tipped to meet him, her need matching his own as they built rapidly toward climax. She'd never been taken so roughly, so spontaneously, before. She'd never *wanted* to be taken that way. But now…oh, now, she knew what she'd been missing.

Everything in the world faded away except Chase and

what he was doing to her. His hands, his mouth, his rigid length…all conspired to drive her over the edge.

With a barely suppressed shriek, she came, her body convulsing, her fingertips digging into his upper arms, her teeth biting down on a mouthful of his expensive Italian suit jacket to muffle the sounds she couldn't help but make. A second later, Chase stiffened, following her over and into the abyss.

His chest rose and fell against hers for several long minutes, then he straightened, took a step back, and began rearranging his clothes.

Startled by his sudden withdrawal, and self-conscious of her disheveled state, she hopped down from the counter and started redressing herself.

"We shouldn't have done that," she said, fighting to get her garter belt and stockings back in place without stripping completely and starting over from scratch. "What will your friends think?"

"They'll think we took a little longer than usual in the bathroom," he told her, rebuckling his belt and tucking in the tail of his shirt. "Either that or they'll think we sneaked off to the coat room for a quickie. Which isn't far from the truth."

He grinned, but there was no warmth in his eyes. A chilling sensation crept through her bones, heightening her senses.

"Chase," she said slowly, running her hands over the front of her blouse and sides of her skirt, checking the buttons and seams and even her jewelry. "Why did you do this?"

"Do what?" he asked distractedly, glancing past her into the mirror at her back and running his fingers through his slightly rumpled hair.

"This." She waved a hand, her voice growing stronger as her suspicions grew. "These strong-arm, neanderthal tactics. Following me to the restroom and locking the door. Having sex on the counter while your dinner guests wait and wonder where you are."

"What about it?" he asked, sounding cockier than ever. He finished fiddling with his hair and clothes and met her gaze. "I wanted you, and since you agreed to be my mistress for the foreseeable future, that means I can pretty much have you any time and anywhere I like."

Without waiting for her to respond, he spun on his heel and marched to the door. He flipped the lock, pulled on the handle, then said over his shoulder, "I'll see you back at the table." The door eased shut behind him.

Elena stared after him, speechless and wondering when her life had begun to spin so far out of control.

Yes, she'd agreed to be his mistress. She'd even enjoyed it after the initial uneasiness had worn off and she'd realized what kind of man Chase Ramsey really was.

But what she'd just seen was *not* the man she'd come to know. It was the side of him she'd met that first day in his office, but hadn't encountered since. She'd thought that part of him was gone, transformed into something more, something different, because of their growing affection for each other.

Apparently, she'd been wrong. Terribly, horribly wrong. And she couldn't pretend it wasn't.

Her hands shook as she picked up her clutch, her fingertips as cold as though she'd been sitting in a walk-in freezer for the last ten minutes.

She couldn't do this anymore. Couldn't play the part of

his mistress when her emotions were so much more involved than that. And she *wouldn't* stick around and be treated like a common whore by the man she'd fallen in love with.

Twelve

From the corner of his eye, Chase saw Elena reappear at the rear of the restaurant, skirt the dining area and march straight out the front door. She didn't glance in his direction or even stop to leave a message with the hostess about her premature exit.

For a minute, he considered going after her. Dragging her back to the table, if necessary, and demanding she fulfill her end of their bargain.

But then, he couldn't really blame her for ducking out early. He hadn't exactly been a gentleman with her in the ladies' room.

And that was as it should be. He refused to feel guilty for doing what they'd agreed upon from the very beginning, especially when he knew damn well she'd been just as hot and eager as he had. The memory of their fierce, frantic coupling still rang through his veins, making him want to track her down and take her all over again.

Which didn't bode well for his decision to put their relationship back on the right track. He was finished being led around by his raging libido. Finished being manipulated by wide eyes and pouting lips.

Elena might be beautiful, and she could certainly be both sweet and seductive, but she wasn't worth losing his soul.

Was she?

He watched until she disappeared from sight, then turned reluctantly back to the couple seated across from him. Creating an excuse for Elena's absence, he told the Hasslebecks she hadn't been feeling well before dinner, and that something she'd eaten must not have agreed with her, so he'd called a cab and sent her home. He wasn't sure they believed him, but he also didn't care.

Then, feigning an interest he didn't quite feel, he wrapped up the evening as quickly as possible, put the amount for the entire meal on his gold card and left a generous tip for the server. Parting company with Mr. and Mrs. Hasslebeck in the lobby, he headed for his car and drove home.

He didn't feel remorse for the way he'd treated Elena. Didn't miss having her near or want to track her down just to hear her voice again.

His fingers tightened on the steering wheel, his knuckles turning white.

He didn't. And he was damn tired of her invading his thoughts twenty-four hours a day.

Pulling into his driveway, he cut the engine, slammed the car door and stalked into the house.

He was better off without her.

First thing in the morning he'd have Nancy call Elena and find out if she was still willing to go along with their bargain. If she was, then he'd have to make it clear that he expected her to be where he wanted, when he wanted. No more of this flitting off just because she got her nose out of joint over something he did or said. As his mistress, she didn't get a say in his behavior.

And if she wanted out, that was fine with him, too. It might even be a better turn of events for both of them.

Of course, if that was the case, then his first order of business would be to put the wheels in motion to buy out Sanchez Restaurant Supply.

Either way, he was bound to win.

Too bad he didn't feel like a winner.

He tromped upstairs, his feet dragging like lead weights at the ends of his legs. He loosened his tie and shrugged out of his jacket, draping both garments over the back of a chair as he entered the master bedroom.

His bedroom, although it didn't feel quite as safe and comfortable as it once had. Before Elena had spent the night there…in his house, in his bed.

Even though she wasn't there, her presence lingered. Her perfume, the sound of her voice. He could smell her in the air, on the towels in the bathroom, on the sheets and pillowcases beneath the heavy comforter. He could hear her husky laughter everywhere he went, inside the house and out.

With a frustrated growl, he finished stripping on his way to the shower. Hot water did nothing to smooth the sharp edges of his lousy mood, and cold water did nothing to calm the arousal building steadily through his system.

What did he have to do to get her out of his head, out of his life?

He slapped his hand against the wet tile, letting beads of water pelt him directly in the face, wishing it could wash away the sick, gnawing ache in his gut as easily as it did dirt and sweat.

Just as he was stepping out of the shower and reaching for a towel, the phone rang. He thought about ignoring it, letting it go to voice mail, but at the last minute wrapped the towel around his hips and lunged for the nightstand.

"Yeah," he answered shortly.

"Chase," came the low, feminine response.

He didn't need the caller to identify herself to know it was Elena. His muscles immediately tensed, every cell in his body alert with physical longing.

"This is Elena," she continued matter-of-factly. "I'm sorry, but I won't be able to continue with our agreement. I—"

Her voice cracked, and deep in his chest he felt something crack, too.

"I just can't. I'd ask you to reconsider your plans to take over my father's business, but I know it wouldn't make much difference, so I guess I'll have to live with that. Goodbye."

Her words were strained and tear-thick until the very end, when they turned firm and confident. Chase sat on the edge of the bed, phone pressed to his ear, listening to the droning of the dial tone long after she'd disconnected.

Well, he had his answer, then, didn't he? It was over. She would finally be well and truly out of his life…out of his bed, out of his blood, out of his head.

Which was exactly what he wanted. The sex had been great, no doubt about it, but he could get good sex elsewhere, without all the strings that came with a woman like Elena Sanchez. The last thing he needed was strings tangling up his life.

Returning the earpiece to its cradle, he stood and made his way stonily back to the bathroom. He finished drying off and pulled on a pair of boxer shorts before climbing back into bed and beneath the covers.

With Elena out of the picture, he would no longer be haunted by the past. Finally, things could get back to normal.

He took a deep breath and closed his eyes, ready for the peace he expected to feel to wash over him. Instead, Elena's scent invaded his lungs. Her hair and skin and perfume, the mix of what made her fragrance so uniquely hers, filled his nostrils and caused his gut to twist.

He could strip the bed, leave the room, but he knew it wouldn't help. It wouldn't help because the smell wasn't in the sheets; the sheets had been washed since she'd last slept there. No, the smell—*Elena*—was in his blood and his brain. And maybe even, he suspected, his heart.

Elena couldn't stop crying. Not because of the way Chase had treated her the night before, but because she'd finally admitted to herself that what they had was not going to work. And she'd finally found the courage to call and tell him it was over.

Maybe, if they hadn't had the bad luck to run into Tisha at that party, things could have been different. At least they'd have had more time to see where the relationship was going.

She hadn't expected forever from him, but she would be lying if she didn't admit she'd been hoping for more. More time, more of a chance, just…*more*.

But now it was done, over, and she had to get on with her life.

Inhaling a ragged breath, she blew her nose, wiped her eyes and did her best to retouch the makeup she'd been attempting to apply for the last half hour.

With another sniff, she realized it was about as good as it was going to get. She didn't even bother with mascara, knowing she would simply cry it off in a matter of minutes and be left with black streaks running down her cheeks.

Fighting to get her emotions under control, she left the house and drove to her father's office, glad her sister wasn't around to chastise her for continuing to weep over a man Alandra now considered to be the scum of the earth.

It didn't help, either, that because of her decision to break things off with Chase, Elena now had to sit down with her father and explain that it was entirely possible he was going to lose his business because the extra time he'd been given to collect funds and backers was gone.

Pulling into the first parking spot she found on the street in front of the SRS building, she grabbed her purse, locked the car and headed inside.

The door of her father's office stood open, as usual. She tapped lightly, feeling her spirits lift when he raised his head and smiled widely at her.

"Elena, *querida*," he said, getting to his feet and moving around his desk toward her. "You look lovely today. I'm so happy you came to visit me."

Only her father could make a positive comment about her appearance on a day like today, when both her eyes and nose were red and puffy from crying for the last twelve hours.

Victor Sanchez was on the short side, with a thick,

stocky frame and a generous portion of gray in the otherwise black hair forming a crown around his balding head. He stood two inches shorter than Elena, but that didn't keep him from wrapping his arms around her and lifting her off her feet as he hugged her close.

Elena laughed, as she always did when her father showed such affection for his girls, even as regret poured through her at the pain she was about to cause him.

"Papa," she said reluctantly when he pulled away, tears once again stinging her eyes, "I need to talk to you."

The joy on his face faded slightly as he sensed her inner turmoil. "Of course, of course."

He led her to a couple of chairs in front of his desk and sat down, urging her to do the same, still holding one of her hands. "Now tell me, *hija,* what has stripped the sunshine from your eyes."

"I have some bad news, Pop."

His salt-and-pepper brows met, his fingers tightening around her own. "What is it, *querida?* You know you can tell me anything."

She nodded, swallowing hard before continuing. "I know I told you everything would be all right with the company, that I worked out a deal with Chase Ramsey to give you some time to get together the money and backers you need to keep SRS afloat, but—"

She swallowed again, what she needed to say sitting in her chest like an anchor, pressing down on her heart.

"The…agreement…fell through." Her throat closed and the tears brimming in her eyes finally spilled over. "I'm so sorry, Papa. So, so sorry. I really did try."

For a few moments, her father sat in stunned silence.

Then he opened his mouth, but before he could speak, another voice cut him off.

"Victor, there you are."

Elena spun around in her seat, both her and her father's gazes whipping to the doorway, where Chase stood with his hands on either side of the jamb.

Her heart went from feeling like a stone in her chest to speeding like a racecar at the Indy 500.

What was he doing here? Especially looking like that.

She'd never seen him so rumpled. His expensive, tailored suit was a mass of wrinkles—and if she wasn't mistaken, it was the same one he'd been wearing last night at dinner, right down to the hastily knotted tie. His jaw carried a day's worth of dark beard stubble and his hair didn't seem to have been combed by anything more than his fingers.

"Chase Ramsey," he said by way of introduction. "I know we haven't met in several years, but I've been meaning to talk to you about Sanchez Restaurant Supply."

He directed his words to Victor, but his glance strayed more toward her.

"I'm no longer interested in acquiring your company for the Ramsey Corporation. I know you still have a ways to go before SRS is in the black again, and if you'd like some assistance in that area, I'd be happy to offer my expertise, maybe even some financial backing."

This time she and her father were both at a loss for words. She stared at Chase, wondering why he had changed his mind, even as she realized she didn't really care.

"I… *Gracias*," Victor managed to stammer. "Thank you. I appreciate that, Señor Ramsey."

Chase nodded brusquely, as though the announcement about her father's business was merely an afterthought, then turned his intense sapphire gaze on her. "Elena, can I talk to you for a minute? Alone."

Dropping his arms, he took a step back from the open doorway, inviting her into the hall. His expression was both wary and hopeful.

Curious and confused, she stood, sparing a quick glance at her father, who looked almost ready to burst with happiness at having the family business out from under the oppressive threat of a takeover. Not to mention the possible assistance of a corporate tycoon who seemed capable of turning straw into gold.

"I'll be right back," she said shakily, then smiled at her father—whether to reassure him or herself, she wasn't sure.

Leaving her purse on the seat of her chair, she crossed the room, her heels clicking a staccato rhythm that matched the erratic beat of her heart.

She kept her eyes averted as she slipped past Chase, who towered in the doorway, and waited while he pulled the door closed. He wrapped a hand around her elbow and guided her a little ways away, sending a shock of sensations up her arm.

It was sad, she thought, that he could still have such an effect on her when she'd decided just yesterday to be finished with him. She should be immune to him already, shouldn't she? She should have cut off any feelings for him and built an impenetrable wall around her heart.

And maybe, if he hadn't waltzed into her father's office thirty seconds ago and done something so sweet, so generous, so completely out of character, she could have *stayed* mad at him.

Clearing her throat, she lifted her head and met his gaze. "That was very kind of you, thank you." And then, because she had to know, "What made you change your mind?"

"You did," he said, his fingers tightening where they still held her elbow before suddenly releasing her and letting his arms fall to his sides.

"After you left the restaurant last night, I went home, thinking everything was fine. Better than fine. I knew you were through with our agreement, through with me, and I was *relieved,* because ever since we started spending time together, I haven't felt like myself."

Running his hands through his hair, he blew out a harsh breath. "When you first walked into my office, I wanted to hate you, Elena. I relished the opportunity to punish you for how you made me feel twenty years ago in front of your friends."

"I'm sorry about that," she told him solemnly. "I've already tried to apologize—"

He shook his head, waving off her words. "I know. It doesn't matter. See that's the thing—I thought it did. For twenty years, I couldn't get the night of that Christmas party out of my head, and when you came to me with the request to help save your father's business, I reveled in the possibility of finally getting back at you."

She opened her mouth to speak again, but he cut her off.

"Then there was last night. I treated you with less than a hundred percent respect at dinner, pushing you, trying to put what was between us back on an even keel. What I considered an even keel, anyway," he added with a shrug. "You didn't appreciate my behavior and walked out— which is exactly what you should have done, and no less than I deserved. And after you called, told me our deal was off, I thought I'd feel better. I expected this weight to lift from my chest and my world to right itself again. Instead, I couldn't sleep. I could barely breathe."

Reaching down, he caught her hands, folding them within his own and giving her fingers a squeeze. "I could smell you in the room, hear your voice whispering in my ear. And despite everything I'd told myself, everything I *thought* I felt, *thought* I believed, *thought* I wanted, I suddenly realized what an idiot I've been. Because what I really wanted was for you to be right there beside me, in my arms. That's what I *want*. Now and forever."

Elena blinked, almost feeling the need to clean her ears and ask him to repeat what he'd just said. Her insides were quaking. She was moved and yet extremely wary.

Last night, he'd treated her as nothing more than his paid companion—albeit paid with a favor to her father rather than money. Now, he seemed to want more, he seemed to be saying he cared for her.

But how could she be sure? How could she know that he wouldn't change his mind the next time they ran into Tisha Ferguson-McDonald or someone just like her?

Her brain was telling her to be careful, to proceed with caution and maybe even make him suffer a little bit, make him earn her forgiveness.

Her heart was telling her to throw her arms around him, hug him tight and never let go.

She decided to opt for a reaction somewhere in between.

Ignoring the flutter of nerves in her belly, she steeled her voice and asked, "What are you saying, Chase?"

His hands tightened on hers as he readjusted his hold, linking their fingers together. He yanked her a step closer, staring down at her with the most intense, sincere expression she'd ever seen on his face.

"I'm saying I love you. I think I have since junior high. Even after you turned me down at your family's Christmas party, I don't think I could have been so hurt and angry for so long if you hadn't meant more to me than I cared to admit."

Hearing the words *I love you* on his lips made her pulse pound and her whole body flush warm with affection. She loved him, too. Her feelings hadn't blossomed quite as early on as he claimed his had, but she'd certainly admitted to them sooner.

"But what about what happened the other night with Tisha Ferguson-McDonald? I didn't have anything to do with what she said, Chase, I swear I didn't. And I don't share her opinions or her views. She's an arrogant, ignorant snob."

Her blood was running hot now with remembered fury and indignation. But instead of turning cold and shutting down the way she would have expected—the way she'd seen him respond before—he chuckled. Lifting their locked hands, he pressed the back of his index finger to her lips to postpone the rest of her Tisha-is-the-devil tirade.

"I told you," he said slowly, his tone low and lulling, "it doesn't matter. Yeah, it pissed me off and brought up a hornet's nest of ugly memories I didn't want to deal with and had been hoping were behind me. But it also helped me to realize—a little late in the game, I know," he said, his cheekbones turning pink for a split second as he glanced away sheepishly, then returned his gaze to hers, "that you're nothing like her. Nothing like the women who were with her. Maybe you were at one time, trying to fit in, just as you told me back in Las Vegas. But we all try to fit in when we're kids—even more so as teenagers—and we all do stupid, insensitive things, usually on and off throughout our lives."

He leaned in and pressed a soft kiss to the corner of her mouth. "I can forgive you for what you did when you were fourteen, if you can forgive me for what I did last night. I thought that by pushing you away, I could regain control of my emotions, relegate you to the status of a business arrangement where you belonged. I didn't understand at the time that you were so much more than that."

His voice lowered, seeping into her pores like warm honey.

"That you had gotten under my skin and into my heart. I had to almost lose you before my head cleared and I came to my senses."

Letting her arms fall limply to her sides, he cupped her face and tilted her chin up a fraction. Elena hoped her eyes weren't bright with tears and that her lips weren't quivering with the elation getting ready to spill over from her rapidly swelling heart.

"Tell me I'm not too late, Elena." He whispered the request, his breath dusting her cheeks and fluttering the hair at her temples. "Tell me you feel the same, and that I haven't completely screwed things up with my thick skull and obstinate nature."

For a moment, all she could do was blink. If she closed her eyes, she thought she might faint from such pure, undiluted joy. It all sounded so wonderful, so promising, like everything she'd ever wanted and more.

But she was afraid of getting her heart broken. Of opening herself up to him again, only to be hurt again—and possibly be hurt much worse the second time around.

"What about what Tisha said? What if we run into her—or someone like her—and she acts the way she did the other night? Are you going to hold that against me? Are we going to have to go through this every time someone says something you don't like?"

His lips thinned for a brief moment, but he answered easily enough. "I can't promise I'll be happy about it, or that it won't put me in a bad mood for a couple of days. But I won't take my frustrations out on you; I'll only ask that you put up with me and listen to my complaints until I get over it. I know who I am, though, and I don't need anyone's approval or reassurance."

He ran his fingers through her hair, tucking a few strands behind one ear. "It might have taken me twenty years to figure that out, but I know it now and I'm not going to forget. All I'm asking is for you to give me a chance to prove that. I do love you, Elena. I want you to stay with me. Not as my mistress, but as my wife and partner for the rest of our lives."

A beat passed while Chase studied her face, his eyes blazing like chips of blue ice.

"What do you say, sweetheart? Am I worth the risk?"

He was. Their relationship might not always be easy, but as long as they loved each other and agreed to talk things out, she believed it could work.

"You're a hard man to say no to," she said softly, blinking back tears and sucking air into lungs that felt as if they hadn't been filled for years. "And I do love you, so my answer is yes."

A grin as bright as the sun spread across his face. His happiness spilled onto her until they were both smiling and laughing.

He kissed her, as thoroughly as she could ever remember, and she let herself sink into him. With a sigh, she wrapped her arms around his neck and just barely resisted the urge to pick up one foot the way women did in those old black-and-white movies when every cell in their bodies was being seductively devastated by a man's passionate embrace.

They pulled apart, panting and quickly heading toward overheated.

"So is that a yes?" he asked. "Will you marry me?"

"That's a yes," she said, unable to keep the smile of contentment from her face. Then she reached out and pinched him in the stomach, hard.

He yelped, rocking back on his heels and rubbing at the abused area.

"But I reserve the right to slap you upside the head if you start acting all pouty and rude the way you did the other night."

"Agreed," he said, giving his rumpled shirt a final pat before returning his hands to her waist. "Absolutely agreed. Slap me, kick me, douse me with ice water. But I promise never again to do what I did to you at that restaurant."

She cocked her head and arched a brow. "Oh, I don't know. It wasn't *all* bad. I'll certainly never be able to wash my hands in a public restroom again without having flashbacks."

His grin widened. "Why, soon-to-be Mrs. Ramsey, I think you're a little bit naughty."

Tossing her hair over one shoulder, she smiled back at him and pressed the front of her body against the long, solid warmth of his.

"What can I say?" she returned with all the mischief she could muster. "I've had a lot of practice recently. And I learned from the best."

Epilogue

Christmas music played softly in the background while approximately fifty guests, family and friends, drank and laughed and mingled. The elegant ballroom was decorated with golden ornaments, silver snowflakes and garlands of holly strung across the top of every window and doorway. In one corner a giant Douglas fir twinkled with a thousand tiny yellow lights.

Off to the side, near a long table set with a punch bowl and platters of colorful cookies, Elena stood with her hand clasped in Chase's. She wore a simple white dress that fell to mid-calf, and carried her bouquet of white roses with a single bright red poinsettia in the center. On her left hand, a princess-cut diamond and brand-new gold band sparkled.

It was her wedding day, and she'd never been happier.

She'd never seen Chase look more handsome or content, either.

He'd been the one to suggest they get married on Christmas Day, and hold both the ceremony and reception at her father's house—in the same room as the Christmas party he'd attended all those years ago.

She'd argued strenuously against it, afraid it would tear open too many wounds, stir up too many old feelings they were just starting to put behind them. But he'd been adamant and she'd finally given in.

She was still surprised the day had gone off without a hitch—and that Chase hadn't gotten cold feet at the last minute. But then she felt guilty for even thinking that way.

Tipping her head to the side, she glanced up at her new husband and smiled when he turned to meet her gaze. He leaned down and pressed a kiss to her mouth—something he'd been doing on a regular basis since the minister had said "You may now kiss the bride" only a few hours ago.

"Merry Christmas, Mrs. Ramsey," he murmured as he straightened.

"Merry Christmas, Mr. Ramsey," she returned.

He wrapped his arm around her waist and tugged her close to his side. She leaned her head back on his shoulder, watching their friends and relatives enjoying themselves, even though they'd sacrificed their own holiday plans to be with her and Chase on their special day.

Her father was dancing with Chase's mother? His brother and sister-in-law were standing close, their arms wrapped around each other in an imitation of slow dancing, but they seemed to Elena to merely be swaying back and forth while they exchanged soft, intimate kisses. Chase's father was doing a two-step with a few exaggerated bounces to amuse baby Amelia, who giggled and cooed in delight. And Alandra, of course, was moving around the room, dancing with the eligible bachelors who caught her eye.

Their families got along stupendously, much to Elena's relief. And thanks to Chase not only offering advice to her father on how to rescue SRS from certain doom, but jumping in with both feet and actually becoming a partner in the business, Sanchez Restaurant Supply was doing almost better than it had in its heyday.

"We should probably be dancing ourselves," Chase said above her ear. "People will start to talk if all we do all night is stand here looking stiff and dopey."

She chuckled, then twisted around and began to walk backward onto the dance floor. "I suppose you're right. Christmas carols are an odd choice for a wedding reception, but then, so is a Christmas wedding."

When they reached an open area, he pulled her into his arms, holding her tight as they moved to the more energetic beat of "Jingle Bell Rock."

"It's not odd, it's romantic. And think of it this way— I'll never forget our anniversary. If I do, you have my permission to divorce me and demand I give you everything I own as alimony."

"You're darn right you better not forget our anniversary," she told him, poking him none too gently in the chest. "Especially when all of this was your idea."

When he didn't say anything more for several seconds, she asked, "You aren't sorry, are you? That we had the wedding here, at this time of year? You know, considering."

"What? You mean because this is the site of my abject

humiliation back when I was a sensitive, impressionable teenager?"

He looked down at her for a moment, his expression so serious, she was sure they were about to have the first blow-up of their married lives. Then he grinned and relief washed over her.

"No, I'm not sorry. I wanted to marry you here, on Christmas Day, so that you would know I've well and truly put the past behind me. Besides, if it hadn't been for what you said to me that day, I wouldn't have spent the next twenty years hating you."

She rolled her eyes at that, but he ignored her and continued.

"And I wouldn't have blackmailed you into going to bed with me, and we wouldn't have fallen in love. If anything, I should be thanking you for being a conceited, snobbish little prima donna, trying to impress her friends by stomping on my tender, youthful heart."

He said it with such suppressed glee that she almost reached out to smack him on the back of the head. And wouldn't that be a lovely thing for their guests to witness on their wedding day? Not to mention the photographer, who—while circumspect—seemed to be catching on film everything that happened in the room.

"I thought you said you forgave me for that," she pointed out, taking the opportunity to step on his foot "accidentally on purpose" as they made a semi-difficult turn.

His eyes glittered in the dim lighting, letting her know just what a wicked, dangerous man she'd married.

"Oh, I do forgive you," he said. "That doesn't mean I won't rub it in for a while, though."

She gave a low snort. "Fine. But I'm only going to put up with it for twenty years or so, so you'd better get it out of your system while you've got the chance."

The corners of his mouth curved and he leaned in until his lips brushed hers. "Sounds fair to me."

* * * * *

Happily ever after is just the beginning...

Turn the page for a sneak preview of
A HEARTBEAT AWAY
by
Eleanor Jones

Harlequin Everlasting—Every great love has
a story to tell. ™
A brand-new series from Harlequin Books

Special? A prickle ran down my neck and my heart started to beat in my ears. Was today really special?

"Tuck in," he ordered.

I turned my attention to the feast that he had spread out on the ground. Thick, home-cooked-ham sandwiches, sausage rolls fresh from the oven and a huge variety of mouthwatering scones and pastries. Hunger pangs took over, and I closed my eyes and bit into soft homemade bread.

When we were finally finished, I lay back against the bluebells with a groan, clutching my stomach.

Daniel laughed. "Your eyes are bigger than your stomach," he told me.

I leaned across to deliver a punch to his arm, but he rolled away, and when my fist met fresh air I collapsed in a fit of giggles before relaxing on my back and staring up into the flawless blue sky. We lay like that for quite a while, Daniel and I, side by side in companionable silence, until he stretched out his hand in an arc that encompassed the whole area.

"Don't you think that this is the most beautiful place in the entire world?"

His voice held a passion that echoed my own feelings, and I rose onto my elbow and picked a buttercup to hide the emotion that clogged my throat.

"Roll over onto your back," I urged, prodding him with my forefinger. He obliged with a broad grin, and I reached across to place the yellow flower beneath his chin.

"Now, let us see if you like butter."

When a yellow light shone on the tanned skin below his jaw, I laughed.

"There…you do."

For an instant our eyes met, and I had the strangest sense that I was drowning in those honey-brown depths. The scent of bluebells engulfed me. A roaring filled my ears, and then, unexpectedly, in one smooth movement Daniel rolled me onto my back and plucked a buttercup of his own.

"And do *you* like butter, Lucy McTavish?" he asked. When he placed the flower against my skin, time stood still.

His long lean body was suspended over mine, pinning me against the grass. Daniel…dear, comfortable, familiar Daniel was suddenly bringing out in me the strangest sensations.

"Do you, Lucy McTavish?" he asked again, his voice low and vibrant.

My eyes flickered toward his, the whisper of a sigh escaped my lips and although a strange lethargy had crept into my limbs, I somehow felt as if all my nerve endings were on fire. He felt it, too—I could see it in his warm brown eyes. And when he lowered his face to mine, it seemed to me the most natural thing in the world.

None of the kisses I had ever experienced could have even begun to prepare me for the feel of Daniel's lips on mine. My entire body floated on a tide of ecstasy that shut out everything but his soft, warm mouth, and I knew that this was what I had been waiting for the whole of my life.

"Oh, Lucy." He pulled away to look into my eyes. "Why haven't we done this before?"

Holding his gaze, I gently touched his cheek, then I curled my fingers through the short thick hair at the base of his skull, overwhelmed by the longing to drown again in the sensations that flooded our bodies. And when his long tanned fingers crept across my tingling skin, I knew I could deny him nothing.

* * * * *

Be sure to look for
A HEARTBEAT AWAY,
available February 27, 2007.

And look, too, for THE DEPTH OF LOVE
by Margot Early,
the story of a couple who must learn that love comes
in many guises—and in the end it's the only thing
that counts.

Silhouette®

Desire

Millionaire of the Month
Bound by the terms of a will,
six wealthy bachelors discover
the ultimate inheritance.

USA TODAY bestselling author

MAUREEN CHILD

Millionaire of the Month: Nathan Barrister
Source of Fortune: Hotel empire
Dominant Personality Trait: Gets what he wants

THIRTY DAY AFFAIR
SD #1785 Available in March

When Nathan Barrister arrives at the Lake Tahoe
lodge, all he can think about is how soon he can
leave. His one-month commitment feels like solitary
confinement—until a snowstorm traps him with lovely
Keira Sanders. Suddenly a thirty-day affair sounds like
just the thing to pass the time…

In April,
#1791 HIS FORBIDDEN FIANCÉE, Christie Ridgway

In May,
#1797 BOUND BY THE BABY, Susan Crosby

Hearts racing
Blood pumping
Pulses accelerating

Falling in love can be
a blur...especially at
180 mph!

So if you crave the thrill
of the chase—on and off
the track—you'll love

SPEED DATING
by Nancy Warren!

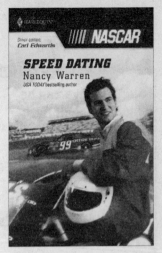

Hearts racing
Blood pumping
Pulses accelerating

Falling in love can be
a blur...especially at
180 mph!

So if you crave the thrill
of the chase—on and off
the track—you'll love

SPEED DATING
by **Nancy Warren!**

REQUEST YOUR FREE BOOKS!

2 FREE NOVELS PLUS 2 FREE GIFTS!

Passionate, Powerful, Provocative!

YES! Please send me 2 FREE Silhouette Desire® novels and my 2 FREE gifts. After receiving them, if I don't wish to receive any more books, I can return the shipping statement marked "cancel." If I don't cancel, I will receive 6 brand-new novels every month and be billed just $3.80 per book in the U.S., or $4.47 per book in Canada, plus 25¢ shipping and handling per book and applicable taxes, if any*. That's a savings of almost 15% off the cover price! I understand that accepting the 2 free books and gifts places me under no obligation to buy anything. I can always return a shipment and cancel at any time. Even if I never buy another book from Silhouette, the two free books and gifts are mine to keep forever.

225 SDN EEXJ   326 SDN EEXU

Name	(PLEASE PRINT)
Address	Apt.
City	State/Prov.	Zip/Postal Code

Signature (if under 18, a parent or guardian must sign)

Mail to the **Silhouette Reader Service**™:
IN U.S.A.: P.O. Box 1867, Buffalo, NY 14240-1867
IN CANADA: P.O. Box 609, Fort Erie, Ontario L2A 5X3

Not valid to current Silhouette Desire subscribers.

Want to try two free books from another line?
Call 1-800-873-8635 or visit www.morefreebooks.com.

* Terms and prices subject to change without notice. NY residents add applicable sales tax. Canadian residents will be charged applicable provincial taxes and GST. This offer is limited to one order per household. All orders subject to approval. Credit or debit balances in a customer's account(s) may be offset by any other outstanding balance owed by or to the customer. Please allow 4 to 6 weeks for delivery.

Your Privacy: Silhouette is committed to protecting your privacy. Our Privacy Policy is available online at www.eHarlequin.com or upon request from the Reader Service. From time to time we make our lists of customers available to reputable firms who may have a product or service of interest to you. If you would prefer we not share your name and address, please check here. ☐

SDES07

HARLEQUIN *Romance*

From reader-favorite
MARGARET WAY

Cattle Rancher, Convenient Wife

On sale March 2007.

**"Margaret Way delivers…
vividly written, dramatic stories."**
—*Romantic Times BOOKreviews*

---

*For more wonderful wedding stories,
watch for Patricia Thayer's new miniseries
starting in April 2007.*

Rocky Mountain
BRIDES